Also by Craig Gusmann:

ANH NGUYEN AND THE DISCORDIAN

To Dad, Mom, and Marisa. Thanks for everything.

THROUGH DARK INTO LIGHT

CRAIG GUSMANN

Foreword

Until late in 2020, when I decided that yep, I'm taking this publishing thing pretty seriously, I hadn't given much thought to what a short story collection might look like. I read a lot of short story collections—they're one of my favorite art forms—and have written a lot of short stories over the years, but had never considered how they might relate to one another, or what themes I tend to revisit over and over again.

The stories I included here are my favorites that I've written over the past 15 years or so. I learned a lot about myself putting together this collection. I learned that I gravitate toward horror and existentialism. I learned that a lot of my fears revolve around the loss of my family, particularly my parents.

And I learned that although I don't always feel as such, I'm fairly optimistic.

This collection is organized to shift in tone as it goes on (hence the title). I wanted to start in the dark, with straight-up horror stories, and end quietly with two friends sitting in a field on the precipice of their lives changing forever. You may also notice a small trilogy near the end of the collection, beginning with THE FINAL DAYS OF FLORENCE and ending with THE PASSENGER. I didn't realize I had written three such tightly intertwined stories until I was late in the editing process of each.

Short stories and poetry allow different types of storytelling. From the experiments in format that stories like NIGHTMARE / DREAM, DREAM / NIGHTMARE afford me, to the removed, dispassionate voice of a story like A BRIEF HISTORY OF THEIR LOVE, or the surgical precision of word choice in DISTANCE that attempts to tell an ultra-focused story that hints at much larger ones around it, these stories have helped me to find my voice. They've illuminated the things I care about, am interested in, and that define me as a writer and a person.

While most of these stories do have a sense of dread, loss, or longing hanging over them, I do think there's a little something in here for everyone. If even one story resonates with you, my reader, then I'll consider these a success.

Enjoy and thank you.

FOLLOWED

Recording 1: September 3rd – 11:38pm – 56 seconds

This feels stupid, but I'm not sure what else to do. I'm driving home from a friend's cabin in Maryland—left our guy's weekend early because my daughter's sick—and something weird's going on. I'm on 476, the Blue Route, heading west. There are three cars behind me. Well, one might be a truck. Like a pickup. Whatever. They've been there, side by side by side, since the highway expanded to three lanes. That's when I noticed the third car pull up next to the others, anyway. For all I know, those first two could've been following me for a while before that.

They're driving right next to one another, in perfect alignment, like they're linked together. And they're keeping the same distance behind me, have been for a while, regardless of what I do. I speed up, they speed up too. I slow down, they slow down. It's been like that for about 20 minutes, since Upper Darby. I have another hour and a half until my exit in the Lehigh Valley.

There's no other traffic. Hasn't been since I got off 95. I keep hoping to see a cop or something. Get his attention. Hell, I'll let him pull me over. But there's nothing. Just me and these three assholes.

I don't know. Maybe I'll just pull off sooner. Let the GPS find an alternate route. I'm sure as hell not gonna pull over to see if they pass. That's when they'll box me in and murder me or something. You know, I wonder if this is like a gang initiation thing. I've read about that shit online.

Anyway, I thought I'd make this recording in case something happens to me. Or maybe it's nothing? I've always been an anxious driver. Ever since my Dad got rear-ended driving me to little league. I don't know. I just know they're not giving me a good feeling. That's all.

Recording 2: September 3ʳᵈ – 11:45pm – 28 seconds

This isn't right. I've been driving maybe ten more minutes and I just couldn't deal with it anymore. Even if I was being paranoid, for my peace of mind I was gonna hop off a different exit, maybe take a detour through Conshohocken, when the two cars sped up to get alongside me. The truck got right on my ass. His lights are blinding in my rearview. I had to turn it away. They're blocking me from switching lanes. Their windows are tinted and I can't see who's behind the wheel. How did they know that I was thinking of taking the exit?

Oh God I hope I see a cop soon.

Recording 3: September 4ᵗʰ – 12:01am – 1 minute, 2 seconds

I tried to outrun them. No dice. Then I thought maybe when the route split and where the tolls are something would change, but they just blew right through them with me. It's since gone back down to two lanes, so the car on my right is riding the rumble strips.

[steady sound of tires bouncing over rumble strips]

There was a cop at the toll. They chased us for a bit. Pulled up alongside the truck. But then slowed down. Backed off. Pulled away. Whatever that cop saw wasn't something they were willing to get involved with. I guess I'm on my own.

[sniffling]

I don't think I'm going to get home. Car's in cruise control. They're just keeping pace. Haven't made any moves toward me. Haven't rear-ended me, or crushed my car between them, or tried to run me off the road or anything. I guess I'll drive until I run out of gas. Maybe they'll get bored of me, go find someone else to harass.

I shouldn't say that.

I shouldn't wish my situation on someone else.

[deep breath]

But I don't want to be the unlucky one that doesn't get to see his wife or kid again. I don't want to be the one that's subjected to whatever the fuck this is. I know it's selfish and wrong, but if I were given a choice I'd switch places with anyone in the world right now.

[six second silence]

I'm gonna try to call for help.

Recording 4: September 4th – 12:05am – 11 seconds

[heavy sobbing]

Nonononono. [unintelligible] My fucking phone won't connect to anyone. I have five fucking bars and every number I call—even 911—says it can't connect.

I'm so fucked.

Recording 5: September 4th – 12:43am – 6 seconds

I'm about 15 minutes from my exit. If I can't get ahead of them to pull off, I'm going to stop. Right in the middle of the fucking highway. I don't care. Let's see what these fucks want to do.

Recording 6: September 4th – 1:01am – 1 minute, 27 seconds

[ambient noise]
[frustrated screaming]
I couldn't exit. All I could do was sit and watch as my fucking hope flew right by me. I swerved right into the fucking car next to me. Pushed him onto the rumble strips. Hoped that it would free me up enough to hit my exit or at least hit the fucking barrier. Maybe take them with me.

I thought that maybe if that happened, if I could somehow brace myself to survive that, then I'd be able to run home. Just run. Fuck the car. Fuck everything in it. And especially fuck these assholes.

But it didn't work. They pushed back. Straightened their car. Sent me back into my lane—boxed in again. I failed.

For a minute I wondered why they were doing this. But you know what? It doesn't matter. Regardless of how this ends, with me safe in bed next to Alyssa or dead on the highway, they don't matter. What matters is me. How I handle this fucked up situation. My Dad used to tell me that inaction was worse than bad action because at least a bad action, a mistake, was proactive. You were in control of your own fate.

I've lost control. I need to get it back. How I might do that is a good god damned question, but something needs to change. If I do nothing, I have the feeling I'll be stuck on this highway, no one else around but these three vehicles following me, forever. The sun will never rise. I won't run out of gas. I probably won't even get hungry or need to take a shit. I'll just sit here in the driver's seat, following this road into the ocean or wherever it ends up.

So fuck it. I'm gonna stop. I'm gonna stop the car, get out, and stand in the middle of the interstate. I expect them to stop, too. But if they don't, then they can hit me. Drag my car along the highway until it breaks apart. I've made my peace.

Recording 7: September 4th – 1:24am – 2 hours, 37 minutes, 11 seconds

I've stopped. So have they. I'm still boxed in, but now we're all just sitting in the middle of the highway.

I think I'm about ready to do this. But before I do, I need—well, Alyssa, you're the love of my life. You're the best thing that's ever happened to me. I never told you, but before we met I was ready to take a nosedive off a building. You literally saved me without even realizing it. You made me better. Gave me a reason to carry on. You're still that reason. It's just that, well, I think to get home to you I need to walk through the fire. See if I can come out unburnt.

But if I don't, thank you. For saving me. For being you. For giving me Winnie.

[ambient noise]

Oh my little girl. I couldn't wait to get home to you this weekend. Your not feeling well was the perfect excuse to come home early. These guys weekends are fun and all, but somehow you're more fun. Playing restaurant with you. Dancing to your made-up songs. I know that you'll grow up to be a talented musician. I was looking forward to watching that happen.

Regardless of whether or not I make it back to you, please don't ever change. Stay silly. Stay creative. Stay innocent. If there's a silver lining to this, it's that I'll get to die before having to watch the world take its swings at you. In a weird way, I'm grateful for that.

Hopefully someone finds my phone and these recordings. You know this, but it's important for me to say: I love you both. You're my girls. My life.

[ambient noise]

[crying]

Alright. Here goes nothing.

[sound of door opening and closing]

[ambient noise]

Hey! Is this what you were waiting for? I'm here! Get out of your fucking cars and come meet me face to face!

[sound of trunk opening]

Maybe you and my tire iron can—

[sound of car doors opening]

Holy shit…

[heavy footsteps on pavement—two sets]

What the fuck are—

[growling]

[screaming]

[sounds of flesh ripping]

[slurping]

[heavy footsteps on concrete—two sets]

[sound of car doors closing]

[passing sound of three vehicles]

[ambient noise]

***

Driving at night, especially when it's raining, terrifies me. My eyesight isn't great to begin with, and usually by the time night rolls around my contacts have dried out. But the thing that bothers me the most about nighttime driving is other people's headlights. I'm convinced that everyone but me always drive with their brights on.

What irritates me most is the light reflected in my rear-view mirror. If the car behind me is close enough, I have a hard time gauging just how far behind me they are. It spikes my anxiety, especially if we're on a single-lane road and I can't somehow get them to pass me. I start to feel as if I'm being followed.

What should one do if they're being followed by a strange vehicle? Try to let them pass? Outrun them? Outmaneuver them? You can't go home, as that's completely giving up your safe space. You might get stuck, perpetually followed.

This story was borne from those feelings. When I played hockey I had to drive down Route 476 a few times per week, often after dark. It struck me how terrifying it would be to look in my rear-view mirror to see nothing but headlights. To be followed, with no recourse, and no hope.

The first-person narrative provides the story an immediacy it lacked in third-person. First-person allowed me to also use present tense and give the protagonist a vulnerability that would be hard to achieve otherwise. This is one of my favorite stories that I've written, which is why it's first in this collection.

I hope the story raises your blood pressure a bit the next time you see headlights in your rear-view.

You may be wondering why this explainer is before the story instead of after. It's because not only do I want to explain why I wrote it, but I have to explain how to read it.

This story is told from two perspectives, side-by-side. On the left page is the woman's perspective and on the right page is her attacker's. You can read only the left pages, only the right pages, or switch left-to-right paragraph by paragraph. I hope it creates a neat effect.

The inspiration for this is a dream my wife had that I thought would make a fun story. The events of her dream gave me the idea to experiment with the form a little bit.

I have a small obsession with how different people view the same events in different ways. Dreams, being elements of our subconscious, was a new way to explore that idea. What if there were a shared dream space? And what if, in that space, one person's dream might be another's nightmare and vice versa? What if that all happened within the space of the same dream? With that, it felt natural to write the story from each perspective side-by-side.

I think it's a fun story (despite its dark subject matter) and may be something I explore in more detail in the future.

***

NIGHTMARE / DREAM

The world is quiet, even the TV. The colors that flash on the screen signify nothing. Holly watches a comfort show—something with baking. Curled up in her lap, more distinct and vivid than anything the TV might show her, is Shadow, flexing her paws so that her hidden claws gently tug at Holly's sweater. She strokes the cat's head, listening to the content purr.

Then he's there. In the entryway that leads to the front door, the quickest escape from the house. He has no weapons, but he doesn't need any. He has 100 pounds on her, maybe more. She freezes.

From the way he flexes his hands and grins, she knows his damned intentions.

Wits returning, Holly scoops Shadow into her arms, leaps from the couch and runs into the dining room. She hears his footsteps following in the hallway—he somehow knows the layout of the house. Shadow struggles and hisses in her arms. Forced to drop her,

DREAM / NIGHTMARE

The world outside her house is quiet. The multi-colored glow of the television softly lights the girl he watches through the window. She looks content. Soon she will make him content. Removing his tools from his jacket, Luke picks the front door's lock as quietly as he can. Confident she doesn't hear him, he enters her home, the familiar feeling of power warming his blood.

Of course she's surprised to see him. They always are. If they weren't, was it a good dream? She's tiny. Or maybe it's the baggy pajamas and fat cat in her lap that make her look small. No matter.

He smiles at her, hoping she'll have as much fun as he plans to have himself.

The girl lifts her cat and sprints into the next room. A chase is always welcome. His dream provides him familiarity with the house, he pivots into the hallway to cut her off at the dining room entryway. When he rounds the corner, cutting through the kitchen, the girl stands

Holly watches helplessly as Shadow flees into the house. Every woman and cat for themselves, apparently. She slides into the corner, far away from the man, trying to decide on a next step.

There is no exit from the dining room except the way she came. Holly moves back toward the living room (if she's quick enough she can get to the front door and, maybe, to some sort of safety), but before she makes it to the single step separating dining room from living room, he has her by the hair and yanks her backward. This is it. She's caught. Her only hope now is to wake from this nightmare.

A hiss flies over her head and onto her attacker's shoulder. A flurry of dark fur and red claw forces the man to let her go. She crawls into the living room, turning to see him flail with Shadow tearing at his face.

Shadow, her savior, has her back claws buried into his shoulder as her front claws tear flesh from the side of his face. He screams, blood gushing from the lacerations.

Then, with one sweeping motion, he flings Shadow across the room. She slams into the wall, falls to the ground, and lies still.

A new emotion rises in Holly. She stands, glaring from poor Shadow's prone body to her bleeding tormentor. She thinks that if he cowers or runs, she'll grieve. Instead, he grins.

She reaches for the nearest weapon—a lit candle—and whips it at him with all her strength. It slams into his near the corner of the room, panting. The cat is gone. He wants to tell her not to fight. He'll be gentle. He's a nice guy. If she just lets it happen the way he wants everything will end soon.

But she runs, anyway. That's fine. The longer this goes on, the more satisfying it will be when he catches her. She has to cross the entire room to get back into the living room and, he figures, nearer the front door. Plenty of time to take the three steps needed to grab her hair. The way her head snaps back, like a puppet in his control, nearly gives him an erection. How much longer to play this out? Not much.

A screech comes from somewhere next to him. Before he can fully turn his head, a dark mass of fur and claw launches itself onto his shoulder and digs knives into his face. He lets go of the girl's hair.

Luke stumbles backward. The setback, is okay. This is a minor hurdle. In fact, he likes the fight. Blood doesn't scare him. Even his own blood. This is still his dream.

He grasps at the cat and throws it across the room. It slams into the wall and crumples. He turns back to the girl.

And he finds her changed. She no longer looks frightened. Instead, her face contorts into something that scares *him*. No, this isn't how these things go. He has to take back control. He smiles.

That sets her off. She grabs a lit candle off the coffee table and throws it at his chest. The flame and hot wax chest, the hot wax spilling onto his neck. He cries out, pushing the candle away from him. Holly charges, a furious scream announcing her intentions, and grabs onto his hair. She pulls his head down, dragging him toward the step. He loses his balance and falls forward onto his knees in the living room.

With a fury she'd never felt in life, let alone a nightmare, she swings her fists and legs at him. He cowers beneath her, unable to deflect all the blows or grab her. She thinks she hears him whimper.

The blood from his wounds flows quicker.

And then it's over. Holly wakes up, her heart beating against her chest. Shadow sleeps at her legs.

pour onto his neck, burning his skin. He screams a vulgarity, but she is already rushing him. Unexpected. She grabs at his hair as he had grabbed at hers and pulls him forward. Unprepared for the attack, he loses his balance and falls forward into the living room. This isn't going as planned.

Before he can right himself, he feels a series of blows to the sides of his head and body. The wounds from the cat open more and he is helpless, only able to cry and attempt to deflect the girl's fists.

He watches his own blood pool around him.

And then it's over. Luke wakes up, heart beating against his chest and urine soaking his sheets.

REAL MONSTERS

Every night, after Jane's parents lay her down to sleep, the noises started. Banging and clanking in the wall near her bed. Scratching beneath it.

Jane was certain there was something under there. Something that would reach out to grab her if she left the safety of her bed or allowed even the smallest part of her limbs dangle over its edge.

Sometimes, when she was at the edge of her sanity, she screamed for her parents. Mom or Dad would come to her, slowly, and never together. They turned on the light, assured her there was nothing under the bed, peeked beneath to confirm, and told her to go back to sleep. As soon as the door shut the noises began again.

Eventually, she gave up trying to convince them.

Now she lay in bed, alert, listening to the things in the wall and beneath her bed, wondering when the day would come that whatever was under there would find its way up to her. She pictured a red-eyed, scaly thing with claws and sharp fangs slowly rising up and then reaching for her so fast she wouldn't have time to scream.

BANG

She gasped. Pulled the sheets up over her head. This was a new noise. Louder. And came from further beneath the bed. Past the floor. Downstairs.

Whispered voices. Another new noise—a *creak*—that was familiar to her as the loose floorboard in the living room. Jane sat up just a little bit, careful not to lean over the edge of the bed. Her Princess Anna clock glowed 2:36am.

Someone walked past her bedroom. No, two people. With heavy footsteps. Heavier than she knew her parents' footsteps to be.

Was it a monster? Had it found its way out from under the bed and was now stalking the hallway?

"Check what's in there," a deep voice said from outside her door. Not a voice she recognized. A scream rose in her throat but she suppressed it. There was still time to hide.

Jane swung her feet to the floor and paused. A tingle skittered its way from her ankles to her thighs, like a finger running up her leg. She fell to the floor and kicked, pushing herself backward toward the doorway, away from whatever was under the bed.

The door handle turned.

There's nothing under the bed, her parents' voices repeated in her head. She looked toward the bed, but the darkness and the bedskirt obscured anything that may be hiding under there, ready to eat her or take her to its lair or whatever it was that monsters did.

The door slowly opened. A sliver of light broke through the dark.

She crawled on her hands and knees as quickly as she could. Away from the threat and into the unknown. Glancing backward, she saw a stream of yellow-orange light spread across her light pink wall.

Diving, she parted the bedskirt and disappeared beneath the bed, hoping that whatever she had to face under here was better than what waited for her in the bedroom.

She was right.

She found herself face to face with glowing red eyes, scaly skin, and long fangs. She tried to scream, but the thing's claws covered her mouth before she could suck in any air. It stared into her eyes and she felt like it was trying to communicate something to her.

It spun her around so they could watch the light playing around her room together. Slowly, gently, it released its grip around her face and pushed her behind it's large body. The light bounced closer to the bed, punctuated with a heavy footstep each time. A pair of boots appeared in the quarter-inch between the bedskirt and the floor. There was a rustling above them.

Someone checking the bed for a little girl.

Finding her missing, the intruder knelt down next to the bed. The light turned toward the space underneath. The intruder's hand pulled up on the bedskirt and the flashlight he held filled the space beneath, blinding Jane.

She didn't need to see to know what happened next. There was a growl. A gasp. A struggle. The light went out and all was dark. She felt something brush past her and disappear somewhere. Her eyes adjusted to the night and she was alone.

Carefully crawling from beneath the bed, she checked the room for signs of other monsters. All was clear.

The sound of sirens coming nearer broke through the quiet.

"Paul? Where are you? We gotta go!" a second man's voice called out from the hallway. Then his footsteps ran from the upstairs to the downstairs and then out the front door.

Jane turned back toward her bed. The bedskirt hung limp, a pair of glowing red eyes watching her through them. They disappeared as whatever lived beneath her bed turned away.

***

My childhood bedroom was in the front of our house, which meant that the streetlight on the curb threw a lot of light into my windows. At night everything created shadows that, to my overactive imagination, belonged to monsters. I distinctly remember something in my room creating a shadow I was convinced was a dinosaur. Luckily, it was a type of dinosaur I knew to be a herbivore.

Not all of the shadows felt as safe. Many forced me under the covers, convinced that I wouldn't last the night.

Those memories were the genesis of this story, originally written years ago. But, I also wondered, what would a child do when faced with a real threat? Would they be able to conquer their fears of an imaginary one?

It's a simple story, told simply. I wanted to layer in a few twists and turns and end on a hopeful note that not all things we're afraid of are bad. Not too bad for just over 800 words.

A NIGHT NOT TO END

1:37am

"These are the nights I wish never had to end," I told Molli, sincere despite the look she gave me. I raised my eyebrows and took another swig of beer. She puffed on the joint, then held it out to me. "You don't believe me."

"It's not that I don't believe you. It's just that I think guys like you will say a lot of things to girls like me that they mean in the moment."

I nodded through my own hit. "I'm serious. You don't feel it? Nothing to do with my being attracted to you, although I am." I smiled, trying to read her reaction. Credit to her, she had a good poker face. "There are just times when you're so content with the company you're in, the place you're in, that you don't want it to end."

"Yeah. I know the feeling."

2:06am

The beer was almost gone. "Nowhere is open," I told Marlon, our host.

"Shit," he said. The music coming from the living room made it clear that people weren't ready to let the party die down. A drunk girl crawled on hands and knees toward the bathroom. Half the party danced, while the other half hung out in corners discussing topics they knew very little about with the confidence only alcohol brings. Marlon sulked into the living room, defeated, knowing that without booze the party would grind to a halt.

"No beer is a good reason for the night to end," Molli said.

"Feel free to end it whenever you're ready," I replied. "A lack of libation won't stop me from getting to know you."

There was something sinister in her smirk, then. If only I could have brought myself to care what that something might be.

3:30am

Of those that stuck around after the alcohol ran out, many had fallen asleep. Cradling one another on the couch. One passed out halfway up the stairs. I wondered if the girl crawling toward the bathroom had made it. I couldn't recall seeing her since then.

Molli and I stayed at the kitchen table. She was out of weed so we shared cigarettes. I was sobering up from the water that I was forced to drink as a replacement for the beer.

"How are you feeling?" she asked. Probably a trick of the light, but her eyes seemed to sparkle with the question.

"Excellent," I said.

"Still want this to continue?"

"I said what I meant and I meant what I said."

She lifted her eyebrows, shook her head, and reached for the pack of cigarettes between us. "You're cute."

4:02am

"The sun will be up in another hour or so," she said. My eyelids were heavy and the first pangs of hunger had hit. For her part, she looked as fresh as she had when I had met her nearly six hours before.

"Watching the sunrise with you will be nice," I said.

"But wouldn't that mean the night's over? We'll get up from this table, the sun will rise, everyone will wake up, and routine will creep back into our lives. There won't be any other choice."

"I guess not," I said. "It's regrettable that we can't just stop time until we're ready for it to move forward again."

"Yeah," she said. "Regrettable."

"I'll be right back," I said. "Don't go anywhere." Hunger could be ignored. Tiredness fought off. But there was no defense against my bladder.

The crawling drunk girl was asleep on the floor in front of the bathroom. I wondered if she had fallen asleep before or after she reached the toilet. One mystery solved, another to take its place.

As I drained my main vein, I thought about the nooks and alleyways my conversation with Molli had explored over the course of the night. Identified areas where I was as charming as I could ever hope to be and kicked myself for the times I showed my whole ass. In total, pretty even. I was clearly doing something right. She was still there, waiting for me at the kitchen table. Ready to fight the sunrise.

I opened the bathroom door and stumbled into the hallway. The drunk girl was gone. In the living room I heard voices and music playing. I recognized the song from earlier in the night. This girl must've woken up and wanted to keep the party going. Chuckling at the thought, I walked into the living room.

Everyone was there. Fresh faced. Beers in hand.

Past them, still sitting at the kitchen table, watching me, was Molli. I went to her.

"Did someone bring more beer?" I asked. "Does some liquor store I don't know about open at four?"

Molli shook her head, then nodded toward the clock behind me.

1:37am

"These are the nights you wish never had to end," she said. "I like you. I want to grant your wishes."

No way. Impossible. "Good one," I said. "How'd you get these guys to go along with you?"

"There's nothing to go along with. You don't want the night to end. It doesn't have to."

I laughed. Not only was she beautiful, and smart, and witty, but she had a knack for practical jokes. "Okay. Well, when the sun comes up in another hour are you still gonna watch it with me?"

"If you want to watch the sunrise, we have more than an hour to wait. But I'm a little confused by your sudden change in heart."

I slid a cigarette from the pack between us and lit it up. "Well, while we wait tell me about your favorite album."

2:05am

My head bobbed toward my chest, jolting me awake. "Getting tired?" Molli asked. "You gonna make it?"

"Yeah, I'm good. Bit hungry, though. What do you say we get some breakfast soon? There's a diner down the street that opens at 5:30."

Marlon approached me from the living room, worried. "Did you bring more beer?"

I hesitated. If this was a practical joke, it was a damned good one. And she had coordinated it fast. I couldn't have been away from the kitchen for more than two or three minutes. "I'm surprised you're awake. You looked as done as a burnt dinner when you went to bed."

"What are you talking about?" Marlon asked. "Dude, we're almost out of beer. Did you bring more?"

I glanced at Molli. That smile was still there. Something sinister still behind it.

"No. I didn't."

"Do you know where we can get more?"

I was speechless. Marlon shook his head and skulked back into the living room, no doubt to tell the other partygoers of the dire booze situation.

Before Molli could speak I whipped my phone from my pocket. Its screen said 2:06am. "How…"

I leapt from the kitchen table and ran to the back door. Throwing it open I stepped into the yard, expecting to see a nascent pink and orange hue as the first rays of sun crested over the houses of the neighborhood.

But it was dark. The only lights the sickly yellow glow from the kitchen window.

Molli appeared behind me. "You wished for the night not to end. So it won't. I'll do that for you."

I spun toward her. She really was something else, this one. "I meant it," I said.

"Then come back inside. Sit with me. Enjoy the night."

We went back inside, together.

***

When I was in my early twenties there were parties to go to every weekend. And if there wasn't a party in Buffalo, there were bars on every other corner (usually the ones not already occupied by a church). Some of my favorite memories of that time in my life, insofar as I have memories of those nights, was the unplanned and unexpected conversations with strangers. I loved sitting at a filthy, beer-stained and ash-littered table in some small apartment getting to know someone.

I remember often feeling like I never wanted the night to end, especially if a cute girl was involved.

I think that feeling of wishing a night could go on forever is a pretty universal feeling. But, like anything we might wish, what are the actual consequences of that wish coming true?

I tried to explore that with this story. The elation, confusion, horror, and resignation that realizing a night will continue as long as you want it. I hope it captured some of those feelings for you.

THE SECRET MONSTER

I first heard it when I was twelve. A midnight whisper in my ear as I lay in bed. A crunching, clicking voice—like a thousand cockroaches being crushed underfoot—belonging to an ancient, elemental creature. Something that my child-brain knew had existed long before me, and would continue to exist long after me. The air changed, became uncomfortably warm, and was filled with the smell of decomposition. It reminded me of the compost bin my teacher kept behind the school.

"She resents you," it said in a language I didn't speak but fully understood.

I sprung up, searching the room for the voice, not convinced that it wasn't some artifact from an interrupted nightmare. Next to me, crouched near my nightstand, was a dark figure. I blinked, certain that it was some devious shadow cast from a mundane object in my room.

It wasn't. Whatever it was had a definite, physical form. There was weight to it. Power.

I wanted to scream, to run or hide, but flight felt useless. This thing was close enough that even if I tried to flee, I'd never make it to the door before being overtaken.

"She resents you," it repeated, leaning forward to punctuate its point. The thing told me this in a casual, relaxed way. Like it was stating something blindingly obvious.

"Who?" I asked.

"Your mother."

I've tried to rationalize the scene a million times since that night. It was a nightmare, my own anxieties about my relationship with Mom manifesting themselves in a bad dream. Hindsight may have worked in my favor if it had stopped whispering to me then.

"You stole her youth," it said, and even though my eyes only registered the outline of this dark figure, I knew it was smiling. "If you were to die right now she'd feel relief. She'd be able to do all the things that you've prevented her from doing. She wouldn't have to spend *her* money on *your* food and clothes. Wouldn't have to come right home from work to spend time and effort cooking for someone that doesn't even thank her. She'd be able to bring Felix over to fuck all night if she wanted, instead of constantly turning him down. She'd have her life back."

The tears came and I stopped caring if this thing grabbed me as I scurried from my bed and out the door. I ran to my mother. I asked her if she loved me. If she would miss me if I died. She told me that of course she loved me. Of course she'd miss me. Why would I think something like that?

"I had a nightmare," I lied.

I believed her.

***

I didn't see it again for six years. I had almost forgotten about that night, pushing the trauma deep into my brain. My relationship with Mom had frayed in that time. Once I turned eighteen, I moved out. I stayed out late, hanging with a group of guys I knew from the neighborhood. When we couldn't get into a loosely policed bar, and if we got bored at the apartment, we'd wander the streets until the early hours of the morning, drinking forties. They were the only people in the world I trusted.

Especially Peacock. He was nicknamed that because of a fashion mistake he made in the early days of high school, a jean jacket with a large rainbow stitched on the back he had found at a thrift store. Instead of letting it define him he embraced the insult and made it part of his identity. Now he wore torn, bright clothing and had his hair in a multi-colored mohawk. Most people kept their distance when they saw him, but I knew better. He was a good dude, loyal to a fault, and the only one in the group that didn't constantly make fun of me for being short, or having a big forehead, or whatever else.

This night, we sat on benches in front of a closed Burger King. It was maybe 2am. Although the restaurant was dark, the lights in the parking lot were bright. Which is why, at the edge of the light's reach, I didn't initially register the thing in the darkness. I saw movement and became vigilant, worried there was a desperate homeless person that might try to rob us, or some drunk stumbling home from the bar looking for a fight.

But when there was no other movement, I calmed and rejoined whatever the conversation was at the time. Probably something about girls, or booze, or the unfairness of our families. Soon after, the group splintered. One-by-one the guys peeled off, finally ready to face their broken lives alone for a little while, until it was just me and Peacock.

"How are you and Amber doing?" he asked.

"Alright," I said.

"Yeah?"

"Yeah." I shrugged, finding the line of questioning to be a little weird.

"Good, man. Good…" he trailed off.

"You alright?" I asked.

"Yeah. Why?"

"No reason. Just seems like something's on your mind," I said. We were nearing the point in our trek where we'd normally split off, so I slowed down, hoping that if we had more time together he'd open up.

Peacock offered a quick smile. Here and gone in a flash, probably meant to convince me that he was fine but instead doing the opposite. "I'll catch you tomorrow, yeah?" he said.

"I'll be around."

Peacock sped up, following his well-worn path home. When I reached the corner I watched him for a while. He never turned around. Just kept his hands in his pockets and his head down, like he was avoiding my gaze.

For me, the walk home was only ten minutes. At this point in the night I'd be lucky to get three hours of sleep before I had to get up for school. I probably should had left hours earlier. As I walked I felt uneasy. Like someone was following me. At that time, because of the neighborhood and our late nights, I always carried a switchblade with me. I wrapped my fingers around it and instantly felt less vulnerable. Every few steps I'd glance behind me, relieved when all I saw were the streetlights.

Then I caught the smell of compost. Memories of that night in my childhood bedroom overwhelmed me. My head ached. A static voice from the shadows. "He's fucking Amber."

I stopped and whirled around, pulling my blade. "Who said that?" I asked, although I already knew. In the driveway of the nearest house, away from the streetlights, I saw it. Standing still, like before, content to watch me react to its taunts.

"Peacock's fucking Amber."

I inched forward, the tremors in my hand forcing me to tighten the grip on my switchblade until my knuckles were white. The thing didn't move.

"Fuck you," I said through grit teeth. Every muscle in my body itched to leap forward, thrashing the knife, slicing whatever this thing was into its constituent parts.

At the edge of the light, less than a foot from where it stood in the darkness, I stabbed with my blade, aiming for the center of the thing's mass. I had never used the knife on anything living before, and had steeled myself for resistance as the tip pierced its flesh. I'd deal with that emotional trauma later.

Instead, I fell forward into the dark. I stumbled but kept my feet. Spinning around, I searched for where the thing went. My breath caught in my throat, unsure of where it was and how to defend myself. I had overplayed my hand.

I heard a horrible giggle behind me. Like bones in a blender. Following the sound, the thing stood in its same spot, just outside of the streetlight's pool of light. Either it was much, much faster than I was or I had gone through it. Somehow, neither scenario boded well for me. Terror overtook me. I began to tremble and a low whine escaped my throat.

"He's fucking Amber," it said, then disappeared, evaporating into the shadows.

I was alone, again, the entire world asleep but me. I ran after Peacock, desperate to tell him—anyone—what had just happened. Desperate to see the look on his face when I told him what the thing had said. Desperate to know if it were true.

My heartbeat paced my run, an image of a naked, thrusting Peacock on top of Amber spurring me on like a whip to a horse. She moaned with every breath of air I sucked in, faster and faster until my legs gave out and I fell to the concrete, scraping my hands bloody. Peacock was nowhere to be found. Odd, since I hadn't gotten far into my own walk home when that thing accosted me.

I lifted myself off the ground. The thought was ridiculous. Amber was my first serious girlfriend. I loved her and I knew she loved me. She was the first to say it, after all. And Peacock was a good friend. He'd had my back in countless situations, from bullies at school to defending me from being the runt of our own friend group. I trusted him.

There was a house party two weeks later. It was the first opportunity for the three of us—me, Peacock, and Amber—to be together since I saw *it*. I stayed close to Amber all night.

"What's with you tonight?" she asked.

"What do you mean?"

"You're crowding my nuts."

"I'm not allowed to be close to you?"

She narrowed her eyes at me. "It's fine. Just weird."

Peacock showed up late (as usual) and found us right away. "Hey guys," he said. He and Amber held eye contact for longer than I liked. My hackles went up and I did my best to position myself between them.

"Either of you need a beer pong partner?" he asked, oblivious to (or unconcerned with) my posturing.

"I need a break. You guys go," Amber said. She walked away, no doubt looking for a little breathing room away from me.

We got drunk. I felt paranoid and possessive, and knew that it wasn't a good look, but felt powerless over it. Every time Peacock got close to Amber, every time he made her smile with a joke, every time his arm made contact with hers or he put his hand on the small of her back I wanted to tear both of their throats with my fingers.

I stood off to the side, watching them team up for a beer pong game, and I couldn't take anymore. In three steps I was between Peacock and Amber. I shoved him as hard as I could. He fell backward into a group of bystanders.

"What the fuck?" he yelled.

"Back off!" I screamed at him.

Amber pushed me. "What's your problem?"

The entire party stared in my direction. I was crying. "Can we go?" I asked Amber. "Just us?"

She stared at me, her confusion overcome with sympathy. "Yeah," she said. "Let's go."

We walked to my place in silence. When we got to my apartment, about a mile away from the party, she stopped me. "What's going on?" she asked.

My mind raced with a million thoughts that centered on a single, core question: Are you fucking Peacock? But I couldn't bring myself to ask. I couldn't face what the answer might mean What the consequences might be.

There was even a part of me, I'm ashamed to admit, that felt like I should be happy for their betrayal. I loved them both, so shouldn't I want their happiness? Even if it was at the expense of my own? As long as he took care of her, what right did I have to interfere in their affair?

Instead, I reached for her hand. "Can we just be together for tonight? Figure everything out another time?"

She stared at me. I could see the questions behind her eyes. I could also see answers. "Okay," she said. I led her into the apartment and she held me until I fell asleep. When I woke up the next morning she was gone. We were over.

I avoided Peacock for a while and eventually he dropped out of school and disappeared. Last I heard he overdosed on heroine. It feels like my fault.

I never found out whether or not he and Amber were fucking.

***

I didn't see the thing again for just long enough to almost forget about it, but its influence on me had permeated every aspect of my life. Each new relationship I made—personal or professional—was marred by suspicion of dishonesty.

Suspicion that everyone I met was keeping secrets that would hurt me.

After the incident with Peacock and Amber I craved a change of scenery, and only applied to colleges away from home. I was accepted to Purchase, near New York City, for creative writing. It was a fresh start.

At orientation we watched a panel on student mental health. Most of the talking points were about school / life balance, time management, stress coping mechanisms, things like that. My takeaway was that there was a certified therapist on campus that anyone could see for free.

I scheduled an appointment the first day of classes. I knew that if I didn't, my time at Purchase would be lonely.

"What would you like to talk about?" Dr. Tran asked. She wasn't what I had imagined a therapist to be like. Of course, my only comparison was what I had seen on TV. She was young and pretty, maybe in her mid-30s, with dark hair and flawless skin. Her office wasn't stuffy and brown, but clean and bright and modern. Instead of lying on a couch, I sat on a normal office chair.

"I'm worried that everyone is keeping secrets," I said.

Dr. Tran nodded. "Do you keep secrets?"

"Only one."

"A single secret?" she asked. There was disbelief in her voice. It felt purposeful.

"Well, only one big one. But it's not something I can tell anyone."

"Why not?"

I clammed up. She was pushing me toward revealing the thing that accosted me from the shadows. The long silence between us made her realize that I wasn't going to tread that territory, so she moved on.

"What sort of secrets are you concerned about others keeping?"

"Their true feelings. Things they've done that will hurt me."

"Things that will hurt you," she repeated.

"Yes. Like in high school my girlfriend was cheating on me with my best friend."

"How did you find out?"

I hesitated. "I didn't find out, exactly."

"Then how do you know it was happening?"

"Someone told me."

"Someone you trust?"

"No. Not someone I trust."

I continued to see Dr. Tran throughout the year. Over our sessions I began to realize that most secrets were harmless, meaningless things. Secrets were normal, often meant to do good rather than harm, and that if we ascribe meaning to people's actions, seeking a way to confirm our suspicions, we'll find what we're looking for.

It took time, but I built new relationships with my classmates. I joined school clubs in writing and web application design. In the writer's group I met Danica, and in the web design club I met Jonah.

Jonah and I were fast friends. He was a computer science major that had big dreams of building the next world-changing application. He had no idea what this big idea was, but he was positive that when he figured it out it'd make him a billionaire. Then, unlike the creators of other major applications that used their billions to do things like colonize parts of Hawaii and subvert democracy, he'd take his money and disappear, living out the rest of his life in peace and solitude.

I had no doubt that eventually Jonah would stumble on the idea that would make him rich. In the meantime, while he waited for inspiration, we were content to party. We spent most of our time at the bars near campus—The Pub, The Cobblestone—especially The Stood, where we saw live bands almost every weekend. The Stood was on campus, where alcohol was permitted only for those over 21, but that didn't stop us. We made friends in high places and snuck booze every event. Jonah became known for always carrying a flask. He said it was his grandfather's, who had died right before Jonah had started college, and so it held sentimental value. No one believed him.

Partway through Sophomore year Jonah hit on inspiration. He had just learned about gamification in his Psychology courses and wanted to apply that concept to everything—including school. Grades, teachers, classes, even the campus itself could be one big game that slyly challenged students to achieve more. With the game he could push classmates for higher grades through competition; advocate for better teachers and classes with ratings systems; and discover new areas of campus with an augmented reality map. It was ambitious and messy, but there was something to it.

Luckily for me, Jonah needed someone articulate and good with design to help build out the app and sell the idea. I was ecstatic to jump on board.

We worked fast. I handled the user interviews, some wireframing, and marketing copy, while Jonah tapped a few developer friends to help him code. There was a sense that we had something special. Maybe it was the group dynamics, or that when idealistic college students rally around an idea there is a sense of invincibility, but even today I believe that Jonah's vision was what he hoped it could be.

So when I was working late in the computer lab, taking my turn at quality control, and *it* appeared in my peripheral, large and black and featureless except for that dead earth smell, I ignored the thing.

For a long time it let me, sitting still and silent, content to watch me work. Somehow, despite the winter cold penetrating the room, I began to sweat. My mind raced with the possibilities of what it was here to tell me. Were one of my teachers planning to sabotage my grades? Was Danica secretly dating someone and leading me on? Did Mom lie to me about why Dad left, as she had lied about loving me? Was Jonah stealing my ideas?

My fingers cramped up. The deluge of paranoid thoughts ruined my focus, forcing me to rework much of what I was doing. Eventually, I knew I'd have to stop testing and go back to my dorm. Would *it* follow me? Somehow prevent me from leaving the room?

I shut down the computer and turned my back to *it* while I packed my bookbag. Without acknowledging *its* presence, I casually walked toward the door.

"Jonah's an alcoholic."

I stopped, still refusing to face the thing.

There was a long silence. It may have been waiting for me to respond, to ask what that meant or why it mattered, but I didn't care.

I left the room. Nothing followed.

In spite of myself, in spite of the progress I had made with Dr. Tran, it was enough to infest my brain with a termite of an idea, slowly chewing through the walls of trust that Jonah had built. All night I lay awake, wondering why that was the secret it had chosen to burden me with about him. We were all alcoholics. Why was Jonah's drinking habit different? Was it because he was close to me? Was this less of a secret and more of a prognostication? Would Jonah's alcoholism ruin our application?

That had to be it. But that was preventable.

From then on, I became hyper aware of the swigs he took from his famous flask while he coded. The back of my neck burned whenever he suggested we go out for drinks. On weekends, when we'd all go to The Stood to watch bands and get wasted, I'd find myself pushing water on him and trying to find ways to slow his drinking.

"What's your deal?" he asked one night, after he'd caught me moving his half-drunk beer away from him.

"Sorry," I said. "I thought it was mine."

"Bullshit. You've been doing this for months. So tell me, what's the deal?"

I hated conflict. But, in this case, considering the work we'd done together, the stakes riding on Jonah's idea, and my love for him, I decided to face it head on. I beckoned him to follow me outside.

We found a quiet place near the dance conservatory. I sat on the concrete steps. Jonah paced in front of me, arms crossed. "I think you have a drinking problem," I said.

Jonah laughed. "If I've got a drinking problem, then you do, too."

I shrugged. "Maybe. But we're not talking about me, are we?"

"I don't have a problem. My grades are better than yours. Our work on the app is going great. I'm really not sure where this is coming from."

"Just a worry, is all. I never said you weren't a functional alcoholic." I smiled, hoping it would diffuse the tension. Instead, it had the opposite effect.

"What the fuck do you care if I like to drink? It's not detrimental to anyone."

"That's not the point. This is the type of thing that will only get worse. What happens if our app gets big and you get so drunk that you mess up an investor meeting or something? Or you write bad code that cripples the thing because you like to sip from that stupid flask while you're working?"

Jonah's eyes got wide. "My app."

It boggled my mind that after everything I had just said, the bleak future I had just laid out, those were the words he came back with. "Sorry?"

"You said *our* app. It's my app. I own it, one-hundred percent." I was speechless, unsure of what he was getting at. "If you're really worried that I'm an alcoholic that's going to fuck up my own future, then you don't need to be a part of it. Whatever happens with the app, you'll get a piece, but you're not needed, anymore. I've got it from here."

He stalked back toward The Stood. I sat in the cold night for a long time afterward, for no other reason than it felt like I had nowhere to go.

***

Danica and I started dating in Junior year, around the time Jonah and I were in the midst of falling out. She loved me unconditionally. I had my suspicions of it from the way she glanced at me in classes and how she went out of her way to do things for me, but there was one moment in particular that sealed the suspicion.

We were in bed when she leaned over me and the entire world paused. "I'd follow you anywhere," she said.

I knew she meant it.

We had met in our creative writing class. I called her out for plagiarizing dialogue from *Moulin Rouge* and she called me out for being an asshole. She handled my paranoia, distrust, and mood swings with a perfect balance of grace and tough love. Like when I had gotten mad at her about something petty (I honestly don't even remember what it was) and she slapped me. Gently, but still a slap. She literally knocked the pettiness out of me.

Between her love, Dr. Tran's guidance, and hearing from mutual friends that Jonah's app was really coming together, I was beginning to see the thing that haunted me for what it was—a liar. A figment of my own twisted insecurities, made manifest by an overactive, oversensitive imagination. I had spent my life assuming that the secrets people held, the flaws they concealed, were some reflection on me. That the secret, if it were true, meant that my relationship with that person was doomed.

But these were falsities. If what that thing said was true, which I really had no reason to believe, then those secrets had no bearing on me. Even when it told me that my mother resented me, that never meant she didn't *love* me. That she wouldn't take care of me. She did love me. She did take care of me.

And if Peacock and Amber were fucking behind my back, who cares? We were teenagers, our hormones running roughshod over our reason, and their relationship was separate from my relationship with either of them. Regardless, Amber went home with me that night I allowed *its* words to poison my actions. That meant something.

Finally, Jonah was doing well. He hadn't spoken to me in months but was able to procure an angel investor for the application by himself. His outlook was bright and I was the only reason I couldn't share in his success.

All of this is to say that when Danica was asleep next to me and that thing appeared in the shadows, hunched near my nightstand like *it* was when I first saw it all those years ago, I was ready for it.

I sat up in bed, staring into the void where its body blocked all light. "You're a liar," I said before *it* could speak to me. "Nothing you've ever told me was true. You're manipulating me into ruining my own life. It's over. You can fuck off."

Its head, or whatever was balanced at the top of its body, tilted slightly. I got the sense that *it* was amused by my proclamation.

"If you're here to tell me some bullshit about Danica, save it. She doesn't keep secrets from me. There's nothing you can tell me about her I don't already know. She loves me." I could hear the panic in my voice. My face warmed with shame.

Another silence. Dread crept into my bones. I ached all over, desperate to just know what *it* wanted so I could go back to Danica, back to the life I had worked so hard to wrestle back under control.

"God damnit! Just be done with it! Then leave me alone."

The thing in the dark leaned forward. So did I.

"You don't love her."

With that, I understood that everything it had ever said was true.

***

I'm fascinated by secrets. We all keep secrets that we believe, if known, would destroy our relationships. But is that true? Or is the act of keeping a secret itself destructive? By their nature, suspected secrets are unverifiable. How does that change our behavior?

I wrote this story to explore these questions by creating a creature whose sole purpose (and pleasure) is to fuck with people. It exploits our aversion to conflict and fear of hard truths by planting the seeds of doubt in our heads. Although honest communication might resolve the problems at the heart of the story, who has the fortitude to have those conversations? I often don't. Nor do the characters in this story.

I wanted to take a long view of one of this creature's targets. Explore how being told the secrets of those he loves would affect his relationships. The twist at the end, of course, is that every secret is real, but he only knows it when the creature reveals one of his own secrets—which is also the most destructive one of all.

HIT AND RUN

Dylan sped down Route 28 through Nokesville, VA, in his father's Trailblazer, blasting house music through his Bluetooth-connected phone, thoughts of what Vanessa might be wearing soaking into his brain. Was she in a short dress despite the cold, her slender thighs peeking out from beneath the fabric, the promised land hiding only a few short inches above? Was her shirt tight enough to advertise the curves of her waist and breasts? If they drank enough, would she allow him to kiss her lips, her neck, her…

The tightness against his pants downshifted his fantasy. Only ten minutes out from Corey's cabin, he couldn't walk into the party with a boner. Deep breaths. Thoughts of Environmental Science or something equally as boring. Better yet, thoughts of his Environmental Science teacher, Mrs. Januszki. Her swollen, blue-veined ankles. How the back of her neck looked like thick sausages stacked on top of each other. Too far? He didn't want to ruin sex for the rest of his life.

He performed an exaggerated shiver and laughed. Tonight would be a good night. Life-changing, even. Confident that he and Vanessa would sneak off to a room by themselves, the alcohol acting as a lubricant to explore one another's bodies, Dylan's throat went dry with anticipation.

Something came from the side of the road, crossing right-to-left in front of the SUV. Dylan braked hard. The vehicle shuddered. Dylan struggled to pull the steering wheel to the right, away from the animal.

THUMP. A pitiful squeal. The driver side of the SUV lifted twice as something went under the front tire and then the back. The car finally stopped. Everything was still.

Motionless, Dylan's heavy breath was nearly as loud as the bass still coming from the speakers. Shifting to "Park," guilt rose into his chest with the thought that he had hit something living. At least, it was alive a moment ago. No way to be sure now, not without getting out of the car.

He stared straight ahead. The harsh brights, kept on because there were no street lights in this rural of an area, illuminated maybe thirty feet of the empty road in front of him. The moonlight was an umbrella of pale light that cast encroaching deep black shadows from the trees onto the road. Dylan wondered what came next. Did he drive away? Should he check for damage to his father's SUV? He'd have to call him, which would probably mean going straight home and skipping the party—and missing Vanessa.

Something moved in the side-view mirror. His neck felt bolted to his shoulders, locked in place. The hair on his neck raised. A slow shiver coursed down his spine. He forced himself to look.

In the mirror a white and gray dog, it looked like a husky, dragged itself across the road with its front legs, the back ones crushed, bloody, and limp, toward the tree line on the other side. Dylan absentmindedly turned off the stereo. He listened to the low purr of the SUV's engine and the dog's desperate whimpers.

"Oh fuck. Oh shit," Dylan said. "What the fuck…" He had never seen such physical devastation before. Had never seen such pain and desperation.

Dylan tentatively stepped from the SUV, something within him screaming to help this poor animal. But how? Standing next to the car, the dog bathed in the red of the taillights, Dylan was lost as to what to do next. Call the police? Animal control? Where he was they'd take forever to arrive. Hell, he didn't *know* exactly where he was. Somewhere quiet, wooded, and without streetlights. What sort of directions would that be for the police? If the dog hadn't died by the time help came, it'd be in the woods somewhere.

That meant Dylan had to help it, somehow. He took a step forward, then paused. What could he do? The dog's back legs and hips were ruined. He had no idea where the nearest emergency vet might be. He risked driving around with a bleeding, crying dog in his back seat all night, watching it slowly die. The dog was doomed, death its only hope of relief. The best thing he could do, the most humane thing, was put it out of its misery.

He opened the trunk, searching for something he might use to brain the dumb dog, and wishing for the first time in his life that his father was a gun nut. A bullet to its head would be easy. Instead, he'd have to find something heavy enough to kill the dog on first blow. The only thing remotely dangerous in the trunk was the removeable lever of the car jack. Not very heavy, but solid.

He imagined swinging the lever and glancing the husky's head. A fissure splits open and blood pours out, but the dog doesn't die. It cries and begs, trying even more desperately to pull itself to safety, wherever that may be. He swings again, still not connecting with a death blow. Again. And again. All night until his arms are exhausted and his eyes are swollen shut from crying.

He hesitated with his hand over the car jack. Turning back toward the dog, its whimpers louder now, like it had imagined the same nightmare scenario, he found that it had nearly dragged itself fully into the woods.

"Stupid fucking animal," Dylan said. Suddenly overcome with frustration, he yelled at the dog. "Why aren't you with your family? Why are you out here?"

Dylan felt an urge to look at the time. Vanessa was at the party, probably talking to someone else.

"I can't help you," Dylan said as the front half—the good half—of the dog's body disappeared into the tall weeds at the edge of the woods. "I'm sorry."

***

"What's wrong?" Corey asked. Dylan had tried to compose himself before entering the cabin. From the way the small gathering stared, he knew that he had failed. On the couch, drink already in hand and wearing black leggings and a baggy beige sweater instead of the short skirt and tight shirt that Dylan had fantasized, Vanessa looked worried.

"I, uh…" something caught in Dylan's throat. He swallowed hard and closed his eyes, trying to force back the tears. It was a mistake—on his eyelids was the vivid memory of the husky pulling itself across the road, its back legs staining the concrete with a streak of blood. "I hit a fox," he said.

"Oh shit," Corey said. "Are you okay? What happened to it?"

"I'm fine," Dylan lied. "Just shaken up. I don't know what happened to it. It ran into the woods. I think I only clipped it."

Corey put his arm around Dylan's shoulder. "Damn dude. Sounds like you need a drink. I hit a fucking deer coming out here, once. Fucked up the entire front-end of the car."

Steered toward the kitchen, Dylan passed by Vanessa and caught her worried and empathetic gaze. He smiled at her, trying to be reassuring. She smiled back.

Two minutes later, beer in hand, Dylan found a seat next to Vanessa. "I'm sorry for what happened," she said.

The broken dog crawling across the road again flashed in his mind. No, that wasn't right. The image hadn't left his mind since he had stepped out of the car. There were flashes of Corey and Vanessa, of the cabin, of this moment, but the primary thought in his head was always of the dog. "Me too."

"Are you okay?"

"I feel guilty," Dylan said, honestly. "It's a living thing. I can't imagine how scared it must have been. Must be."

"Thank God you only clipped it," Vanessa said. "I'm sure it's fine. Back hunting or whatever a fox does." Dylan watched her take a long sip of beer. The guilt he felt, the nightmarish image of the poor husky, sloughed off his shoulders on the softness of her eyes.

Dylan changed the subject to something about school—they shared an Environmental Science class that he knew she hated as much as he did—and, as the teenagers around them got drunk and the party got loud, eventually moved outside for more privacy.

Sitting close, shoulders touching, Dylan's thoughts swam in possibilities. The blue glow from the moon softened her already beautiful features, while the cabin interior's orange glow behind them framed her hair in an angelic halo.

"It's cold," Vanessa said, shivering to punctuate her point.

She had just offered the opening Dylan had fantasized about. "We should huddle together for warmth," he said. He lifted his arm and she scooched over, leaning her body into his, and rested her head on his shoulder. He breathed in the fruity fragrance of her hair.

"This is nice," she said, turning her chin toward him.

The pressure in Dylan's chest was unreal. His heart felt like it might burst from his body, do a little jig on the railing of the back porch and then fall over, dead and happy, onto the frozen leaves below.

He leaned forward, his lips searching for hers, when his peripheral caught a streak of white moving right-to-left in the woods. His head snapped toward it.

"What's wrong?" she asked, following his gaze.

"Nothing. Sorry. I thought I saw something," he said.

"Like what? An animal?"

He derided himself to think of something clever, otherwise the moment would be lost forever, the taste of her lips a mystery he may never uncover. "Our future together," he said.

She laughed and leaned back into him. Close call. Eyes fully closed this time, he again leaned toward her lips, and heard *crunching* and *crackling* in the woods. Something hurrying toward them. Something fast. Something vicious. Something with malicious intent.

Dylan leapt to his feet and stared into the trees. "Did you hear that?" he asked.

"No," Vanessa said. "I didn't hear anything. Are you alright?"

Dylan squinted, searching for the thing with white and gray fur, and red claws and teeth, dragging itself across the wooded floor, back legs leaving a trail of broken sticks, crushed leaves, and blood, desperate for revenge.

"I'm fine," he said. "I'm sorry. I guess I'm still a little jumpy from my close call."

"It's okay," she said, taking his hand. "Let's go inside. I'm freezing."

They went into the cabin together and were swept into the frenzied drinking, dancing, and singing of their friends. While confident he'd have another chance to kiss her (or more), Dylan knew that chance wasn't going to present itself tonight.

The moment had passed. He retreated to the couch and watched the party play itself out.

As the night died down and his classmates retired to any available open room to make out or sleep, Vanessa joined him on the couch. He held her in his arms as she drifted into dreams, contentment washing over him. Maybe this was the best night he could hope for. They'd eventually find time to explore one another's bodies. He closed his eyes, ready to let sleep overtake him and sober him up.

A howl jerked him awake.

"What happened?" Vanessa asked through a fog, her eyes still closed.

"Nothing, just a bad dream," Dylan said.

She was already asleep. From the couch Dylan had a clear view through the window, past the back porch, and into the woods. Another howl cut through the night, closer this time. Too close. He couldn't see anything past the first few trees. Although the night was clear and the moon was full and bright, the branches of the trees threw too many shadows to be certain that anything he saw wasn't imagined.

More howls. They sounded as if the dogs surrounded the cabin. He scanned the room. No one else stirred. Was it because they were so drunk that sleep made them deaf? Or did they not hear what he heard?

A chorus of barks joined the howls. Then low growling. The growls were close. Maybe even at the front door.

Dylan pulled Vanessa closer to him, prepared to wait out the night, his only company the chorus of howling, barking, and growling to remind him of what he'd done.

***

When morning came and the noises finally stopped, Dylan decided to leave. Exhausted and still drunk, he slid himself from under Vanessa and found Corey in his bedroom, sharing a twin-sized bed with a sophomore girl Dylan recognized but whose name he didn't know. He shook Corey awake.

"Oh, hey man," Corey said, barely able to open his eyes. "You good? Need a drink?"

"It's morning, dude."

Corey shielded his eyes from the sliver of sunlight penetrating the curtains. "So it is. What's up?"

"I'm heading out. Just wanted to let you know. Thanks for the good time."

"No problem. My parents hardly ever come out here when it's this cold. We can do this every weekend if you're up for it. How'd it go with Vanessa?"

"Solid, man. Solid. I think we've got something going. But I really need to go. I'll give you a call later, alright?"

Corey nodded in slow motion, then threw his arm back over the sophomore girl and closed his eyes.

Before going to the car, Dylan walked the perimeter of the cabin. There were no animal prints, droppings, or other evidence that the noise he'd heard last night was anything more than nightmare and guilt. The dog was probably already dead and being picked apart by other hungry animals. Its misery was over. He'd never see it again. Eventually the memory of the night would fade. Eventually he'd be able to decouple the small tragedy with his feelings for Vanessa. His primary remembrance of the night would become their almost-kiss on the back porch and cuddling on the couch.

He convinced himself of these things, and it gave him the strength to drive home.

***

Starting to sober, in the daylight, and without thoughts of Vanessa to occupy his imagination, the drive from the cabin back to civilization was longer than Dylan remembered. The trees all looked the same, blurring together into a streak of muted greens, browns, and grays. Even if he wanted to, he didn't think he'd be able to find the scene of his accident. Shit, at the speed he was going he had probably already passed it.

Except he hadn't. A diagonal streak of red beginning in the opposite lane spread into the one he now occupied. He slowed the SUV like he was an observer of some accident that he hadn't caused.

Seconds later, he was standing in the middle of the road, car idling quietly next to him, staring down at the still slick blood. Following its trail into the woods, he wondered how far the dog had gotten. If perhaps it had found a hole to wait for death, safe from further trauma. Or, by some miracle, it had found its way back home where its panicked family rushed it to the emergency vet. They'd performed overnight surgery, surely needing to amputate at least one smashed leg, but saved the dog's life. The family would appreciate how close they were to losing their pet and resolve to provide it the best life possible.

But Dylan didn't believe in miracles, not really. Still, he hoped that there was some fairness in the world and that it wasn't all chaos and pain.

He took another step toward the treeline. From the broken branches and red stain in the light snow, it was clear where the dog had dragged itself through the brush and grass. To learn its fate, all he had to do was follow.

Dylan hurried back to the SUV and worked the vehicle up to 70mph, getting as far away from the tragedy as possible.

***

"What the hell happened?" Dylan's father said to him the second he had opened the driver side door. "You hit something?"

Dylan circled the front of the SUV. In his eagerness to leave the cabin, he hadn't bothered to survey the damage. The plastic bumper had a crack running from its middle to the front tire. There was a red splotch on the undercarriage.

"Uh, yeah," Dylan said. "I hit a fox."

"And you didn't call or come home?"

"I didn't think it was this bad. It was dark."

His father bent down and touched the cracked bumper. "Damnit. No sense having insurance take care of this. Premiums will shoot up. What should we do about it?"

Dylan knew the answer. He just didn't like it. "I don't have the money."

"I know," his father said. "So what can we do about that?"

"I'll have to pay you back a little at a time."

"Go on."

Dylan worked at Burger King, but most of the money he earned went to hanging out with his friends at restaurants, seeing bands play nearby, and clothes. He had meager savings. "I'll give you what I have in my savings account and then make up the difference every week until it's paid off."

"Okay," his father said. "Go shower before you see Mom. I can smell the beer on you from here."

Inside the house Dylan felt an overwhelming desire to see the family's dog, Maximillian J. Retriever (the name being his younger sister's invention). Max was a six-year old golden retriever and the ideal family dog: well-behaved, gentle, and easily trained. Dylan wondered how he'd feel if it were Max crawling through the woods, broken and alone.

"Max?" he called out, listening for the familiar click-clack of Max's long nails on the hardwood floors. The dog hurried around the corner of the living room and Dylan opened his arms. "Hey buddy!"

Max snarled and leapt toward Dylan's throat. All he could do for protection against Max's fangs was to raise his forearm in sacrifice. Max latched onto it, snapping his jaws shut, teeth puncturing Dylan's skin and muscle, blood pooling in the dog's mouth and dribbling down his chin. Max jerked and pulled at Dylan's arm, dragging him onto the floor. Even with the adrenaline dumping into his bloodstream, the pain was unbearable. Dylan thought he might pass out and be unable to defend himself in even this meager way. "Mom! Help!" he screamed.

Dylan's mother rushed into the room and, without hesitation, beat at Max's head with her fists. "Max! Off!" his mother screamed, as if Dylan's arm was a particularly valuable linen Max had gotten hold of. "Off!"

She pulled at Max by the nape of his neck. He finally released Dylan's arm and his mother kicked at the dog. "Crate! Now!" Max backed away, still snarling, his snout red with Dylan's blood, caught between instinct and the command. After another moment's hesitation, Max complied, disappearing into the den. Dylan's mother followed and locked the crate before hurrying back to Dylan.

"C'mon," she said, lifting him by his good arm. "Sean! We have to get Dylan to the hospital!"

Dylan's father appeared in the space between the foyer and the garage door. "Jesus Christ," he murmured in shock at the blood pouring from Dylan's arm and soaking into the white hallway runner. He snatched the keys from their place near the front door and led Dylan and his mother to the car, not bothering to close the garage or lock the doors.

***

Dylan felt the pull of each stitch on his numb, wrecked arm but couldn't bring himself to watch the doctor work. While evaluating his arm, the doctor remarked that he was lucky—

some attacks required surgery. If Max had gotten to his throat or face, this would be a vastly different procedure.

From nearby he heard his father talking with the vet on the phone. At first, his mother had forced him to call and make an appointment to have Max put down, but Dylan protested until they agreed to figure out why he was attacked before condemning the dog.

"No, Max hasn't been in contact with any other animals recently. Aside from his walks, he never leaves the yard. No, nothing like that. Until twenty minutes ago he was perfectly normal. Absolutely no change in behavior. No stress. Nothing." Sean paused and listened. "I suppose Dylan could have had an odd smell on him. He was at a cabin last night and hadn't showered yet."

When he hung up, Sean came over to Dylan's side of the bed. "You didn't touch another animal last night, did you? Does Corey have a pet that he brought to the cabin?"

"Um…" Dylan said. If the answer were 'no,' then Max would be euthanized. He didn't want that. "Yeah. Corey had his rabbit there."

Sean nodded. "Okay. Well, I don't know what to do."

"Don't do anything," Dylan pleaded. "I don't want Max put down."

Sean looked toward Dylan's mother, who had been pacing by the wall, chewing on a hangnail. But now watched their conversation. She shrugged.

"Max stays in the crate tonight. We'll see how he reacts to you in the morning, when you're showered and things have calmed down. Decide what to do then."

***

They got home late in the afternoon. Sewing nearly 200 stitches into Dylan's arm had taken hours and then he was given vaccinations for tetanus and rabies. Dylan's sister, Olivia, waited with their Aunt on the front porch. "Thanks for keeping Olive company," Sean said. He and Dylan's Aunt stepped away from the porch, speaking to one another in hushed tones.

"What happened to you?" Olivia cried out.

"I fell," Dylan said. He hurried into the house, hoping to avoid Olivia's interrogation.

Dylan stepped into the den and looked at Max through the bars of the crate. Max immediately leapt to attention, a low growl in the back of his throat. Understanding, Dylan retreated to his bedroom and resolved to spend the rest of the night hiding from the world.

When night came, he found himself enveloped in darkness, the moonlight only hinting at the outlines of trees around him. Crawling on the dirt, palms rough and bloody from pulling his useless legs behind him, Dylan was desperate to hide. There were things in the woods that wanted to hurt him. He could hear them. The footfalls rushing past, just out of sight. The whines of hunger. The low growls of an animal working up the nerve to attack.

If he could just find someplace to hide maybe he'd be safe. His family was surely looking for him, as desperate for him as he was for them. They'd find him and bring him home and repair his crushed legs and in time this nightmare would end.

His arms hurt. With every pull they became weaker. Broken sticks stabbed his abdomen as he dragged himself over them. It wouldn't be long, now. With no energy left, no hope of a savior, the end was close. He wanted to be grateful for death, grateful for the pain to go away, but he also didn't want to die. Not like this. Not here, away from those he loved.

A filthy paw stepped in front of him. Craning his neck, he found a wolf staring down at him, licking its muzzle. It bared its teeth.

When Dylan woke he was in the den, sitting on the floor in front of Max's crate. Max lay with paws crossed, silently watching him. A cacophony of barking filled the room. Dylan spun around, searching for the epicenter of the noise, but found nothing. He stood and peered out the front window. Standing in the middle of the road was a white and gray husky. The barking stopped.

Dylan glanced toward Max. The dog didn't move, but somehow Dylan knew what to do. He went into the street and followed the husky.

It led him deep into his neighborhood, the cul-de-sac a confusing maze of roads, houses, and tightly manicured lawns. As he followed the husky other dogs joined. Within four blocks there were ten other dogs keeping in step.

The husky stopped in the road. Dylan approached, the other dogs forming a tight circle around them. He reached out to touch the husky and it snarled. The dogs surrounding them dropped into attack positions, their front legs splayed out in front of them, their back legs ready to pounce. Startled, Dylan leapt back, tripping over his own feet and falling into the road. The husky stepped over him and put its paws on his chest. A line of drool hung from its lips.

"I don't know what to do," Dylan said. "I'm sorry. I should have tried to help. I should have done *something*."

He was crying. The husky stopped snarling and tilted its head, searching for something on Dylan's face. A true sense of regret, maybe. Then, one by one, it looked toward the other dogs. Each turned and trotted home.

Dylan understood.

***

In the early morning light the dull red staining the country road took on an almost otherworldly sheen. The dawn sunlight reflected off the sticky slickness, adding pinks and oranges to its crimson hue. Dylan traced its path into the woods. With a deep breath, he took his first step toward where it led.

He pushed aside the brush and brambles and branches as he walked, each broken stick and blood-soaked blade of grass a small moment in the long story of the husky's suffering. His guilt rose in his throat. With a great sigh the tears came.

The dog had fought for a long time, making it at least sixty yards into the woods. The first clue that he was near where its journey ended was the smell. Death—rot and shit and iron— gagged him. He heard the buzzing of the flies next. And then, finally, he saw the corpse.

Crows picked at the open ribcage some other animal had torn into. Dylan's eyes drifted to the back legs of the husky. They were nothing more than sacks of skin filled with pieces of broken bone. The husky's white fur was stained red from its hind legs up to its chest, where something had taken away chunks of flesh.

Dylan chased away the crows and knelt next to the dog's muzzle. That, at least, was surprisingly clean. Some dirt, and Dylan pulled away the sticks and grass stuck in its fur, but no blood. The crows had left the husky's eyes alone. They were dilated and thick with fog, the dog's last expression memorialized.

Fear permeated those eyes. The same fear Dylan felt in his dream. The fear of dying painfully and alone, knowing that there were people somewhere that loved and missed him and that he also loved and missed.

Beneath the thick fur of the husky's neck was a sky-blue collar. Dylan checked it for a tag. "Alright, Bailey," Dylan said, finding an address engraved on the tin, paw-shaped tag. "Let's get you home."

His arm was in a cast, which made lifting the dog difficult, but after a few tries Dylan succeeded in scooping Bailey into his arms, careful not to spill out his insides, and carried him to the car. He gently laid Bailey onto the back seat, already prepared with an old, comfortable blanket.

Dylan typed the address into his GPS. He looked back at Bailey and tried to imagine what the dog would look like clean and healthy in his back seat. If he had been paying attention that night, instead of fantasizing about Vanessa. If he had been able to stop in time, coax Bailey to him, and then drive him back to his family.

But he couldn't imagine that. It was too far removed from reality.

Dylan wiped his bloody hands on his shirt, shifted the car into gear, and began the journey he should have completed two nights before.

***

This story is the result of several experiences I had while driving. For about a year I drove out to Pottstown, PA to play hockey. It was about a 30 mile drive, with the first 10 or so miles mostly residential and the last 20 all highway. This being Pennsylvania, the highway is elevated in areas, so if something were to dart out from behind the barrier you wouldn't see it coming. Driving at 70 mph, this was a constant worry of mine.

Luckily, I never had that experience on the highway. Where I did have it was just coming off of it onto a main road. There, a deer ran out from the treeline, barely missing my car, and causing the car behind me to swerve. I didn't quite see what happened in my rear-view mirror—I think the deer may have run into the side of the car and kept going—but it was the realization of a long-standing fear of mine. This story really started to take shape after that experience.

Finally, while visiting my sister in Springfield, VA a fox darted out from the treeline. I braked but tapped it with the front end of my car. The fox ran off, nearly got stuck in a fence, and then disappeared into the trees.

I searched for it, guilt eating away at me, but with no luck. I hope that it was just shocked and scared—feelings I shared—but ultimately okay.

The feelings that surround those memories informed the guilt at the heart of this story. It's bad enough to hit any animal and see them suffer. To hit a dog that you know has a loving home cranks that guilt to 10. And that's enough guilt to start imagining things, isn't it?

TOGETHER FOREVER

When the sky finally falls
And the flames rush toward us
We'll be together

I'll ask, "Will you hold my hand
And guide me to Heaven?"
You'll say yes

Our eyes will meet
Our fingers will interlock
And, for the last time
Our lips will touch
As we kiss the world goodbye

***

Like any good speculative fiction writer, I spend a lot of time thinking about the end of the world. Not the slow end of everything that is most likely to happen through climate change or nuclear war fallout (or the "Big Rip," as the next story in this collection focuses on), but the cataclysmic apocalyptic end that's impossible to prepare for. An asteroid strike, being in the blast radius of the aforementioned nuclear bomb (a preferable way to go than the other ways to die in a nuclear war), unexpected volcano eruption—whatever. Regardless of the scenario, my thoughts always return to the people I'd want to spend my last few moments with. If the end were to come I hope I'd be able to look into my wife's eyes one last time.

A COLD, SILENT NOTHING

To visit Dr. Orson, I had to make arrangements with a state-of-the-art mental health facility in which he was under 24-hour supervision. He hadn't spoken to anyone in months, which was an improvement over the nearly incoherent babbling that had consumed him in the weeks before. In those first weeks he spoke of "an eye where existence rests when there is nothing left." No one could reach him or force him to do anything. He claimed there was no purpose. He was relegated to bed rest, a feeding tube, and a bed pan.

My understanding from speaking with his doctors was that since being admitted he had begun to recover, a testament to the man's intellectual strength. Emotionally, however, he was lost. Whatever he had seen changed his soul.

We had never met before I stepped into his room. Even in the good times, before he had traveled to the end of everything, he wouldn't have known me. But I knew him. Physicist, philosopher, time traveler—those were what most knew of his accomplishments. But he was also a writer, an educator, a father, a philanthropist—less flashy, but no less important, achievements. All facets that, in varying degrees, made up his personality. It was a shame that his intellectual curiosity got the better of his emotional reason and, depending on your perspective, his moral compass.

Despite knowing this of him, I stood before him to decide if I should follow in his steps. I wished to see the end of everything.

He sat motionless in a chair that faced the window, his slack jaw and relaxed posture a product of the anti-suicide neuro-mesh that enveloped his brain stem. The early evening sunlight was harsh on his face, but he stared into it, unblinking. Pale to the point that one might confuse him for an albino, he nearly glowed in the sunlight. He was emaciated. I remembered the footage I was forced to watch of his return from the machine and couldn't help but think that he looked healthier as he crawled from it, tongue hanging from his lips and eyes rolling into the back of his head, than he looked now.

"Dr. Orson, my name is Wesley Stephens. I'm here to ask you about what you experienced at the end of everything," I said, speaking slowly and enunciating clearly, as if I weren't speaking to one of the greatest minds to ever live. I watched his face carefully. No change. If it weren't for the micro-movements of his pupils, the tiny vibrations of a soul spinning behind the eyes, I'd have thought he'd died sitting up.

Before entering I had been given a folding chair. Aside from the chair he sat in and a twin-sized bed along the edge of one wall, it was the only furniture in the room. I set it down and took a seat directly in front of him, blocking his view of the window. "I'm asking because I, too, plan on going there. But before I do, I'd like to know what you saw. What happened to make you--" I stopped. His eyes had suddenly focused on me, his pupils snapping toward my own. He held my gaze for a long while before he spoke. Whatever emotional and intellectual trauma he fought was momentarily shoved aside. I had his full attention. The clarity and intensity with which he stared into my eyes unsettled me.

"That's not possible," he said. His voice was gravelly, dry, like it needed to be lubricated and warmed up before use.

"I found a way around the failsafes," I explained. "Permission is an issue, but my colleagues have agreed to support me depending on the outcome of this conversation. No one else will know until its done."

"There will be no outcome," he said, his voice strong. "There will be nothing." He turned back toward the sunlight.

"Sir," I began, choosing my words carefully. Not because he would become defensive if my tone were wrong, but because I held him in such high regard. He deserved all the respect I could muster. "I'm afraid my intentions for this conversation are not to get your permission. If you refuse to educate me on what you saw, why you've ended up here, then I will simply move forward to find out for myself. My hope is that you can prepare me for what you experienced, so that I might come out the other side intact."

His gaze returned to me, the smirk a welcome if disconcerting addition. "You stupid fuck," he said. His crassness and dismissiveness pushed me against the folding chair. "There's no way to prepare for the end of everything. It just is."

"Dr. Orson…" I began. I had a list of arguments and talking points in my head. About the importance of discovering what's at the end so we know how to live through the present. Seeing the future as a way of saving the now. Satiating our immense scientific curiosity! But he immediately shot through anything I might say when he leaned forward and wrapped his frail, bony hand around the back of my head.

"The human mind is capable of a great many things. But it is incapable of a nearly infinite number of other things. Despite what you may think, what power you think you have over your person and the world because we've evolved to understand consciousness of consciousness and manifest beautiful creations with just a thought, does not mean that our brains aren't fragile. I assure you, Mr. Stephens, they are. The traumas we endure as children stay with us through adulthood. And on the scale of the universe, which is what we're discussing, we are still children and will remain children until the end of our species. Do not peek through the keyhole to witness the same trauma I have. I beg of you, let this mystery stay a mystery. There are things we cannot understand, let alone control, and are therefore not worth knowing."

I was shocked to hear this line of reasoning from someone like Dr. Orson. A man who had dedicated his life to understanding the most minute workings of our existence was telling me that there was no way to understand something. That there were things we *shouldn't* know. That our intellects were too fragile to comprehend any aspect of the universe was unconscionable to me.

"That's a coward's rhetoric," I said, standing. "The entire history of humanity is the pursuit of greater understanding in service of bettering ourselves. It's how we tamed the wilderness, conquered the stars, and expanded our footprint across the galaxy."

"How arrogant and small-minded you are. This," Dr. Orson said, gesturing to the space around him, "Isn't the abode of an insane man, but the home of an enlightened one. And if you travel to the end, you'll learn the same difficult lesson I have. You'll join me here to live in our enlightenment and nothing else until we're allowed to die." He raised his voice with the last statement, intending it more for the doctors he knew were watching than for me.

"Maybe so," I said. "But the ravings of a lunatic about children and trauma aren't persuasive. Thank you for your time, Dr. Orson. I do hope the best for you."

Dr. Orson returned to his statue-like state, as if our entire conversation was something that had occurred only in my mind. Perhaps it had. Knowing what I know now, there is much about reality I no longer understand.

***

The machine was inelegant. It was beautiful in its own way, but had unsightly thick wires running along the floor that led into large electrical ports. The heat the machine generated would incinerate anything inside its domed head were it not for the faraday cage beneath its rubber skin.

Walking into the room I imagined that I was about to enter a giant, blind octopus's maw. Everyone called the machine CHAUCER, after the medieval poet that wrote of righteous travelers, but I never liked the name, though I understood the reasoning.

Bill and Neil watched on a remote feed from a location several miles away. The machine required so much energy and there was so much that could go wrong, it was safest for anyone that wasn't a traveler to be outside of any potential blast radius. That's why CHAUCER was built in the desert, 30 stories underground, only connected to the outside world via the cables and video feeds that Neil and Bill now used to monitor me. Otherwise, I was alone with CHAUCER.

Neil's voice came from the speakers built into the wall above the machine. "I think you should turn back. Aside from the danger to you, if we get caught…"

"We'll only get caught if the three of us can't keep a secret for another hour. After that, it'll be done and it won't matter. I'll have the knowledge. They won't be able to take that away."

"If you don't end up like Dr. Orson," Bill interjected.

"He's not the man any of us thought he was," I said, wincing at my own blasphemy.

There was a long silence over the intercom. I didn't blame them for not believing me. I didn't believe myself. Not fully.

It's a different thing to watch your idol crumble from their pedestal. Even more so when you're the one holding the sledgehammer.

There was no special suit to wear, no additional precautions to take. CHAUCER was designed to operate remotely, safely, with the traveler's only responsibility to do just that—travel. I climbed inside the contraption.

The inside of CHAUCER was spacious, its walls smooth and dark. When I pulled down the door behind me the area became pitch black and silent. Because of the faraday cage that acted as the skeleton of this octopus (if you'll forgive the inaccuracy in service of metaphor), there were no electrical signals coming in or out. Neil and Bill had no way to communicate or monitor me.

And I had no way to turn back.

There was no way to prepare for travel. On my other journeys it had been instantaneous; I stepped into the machine and after a few moments of blackness the time I was sent to study popped into existence. I did some of the classics early on—the signing of the Declaration of Independence, the moon landing, the construction of the Great Pyramids—but eventually turned to more esoteric moments. Small moments of emotion that connected all of us across oceans, across cultures, and across time.

I became obsessed with the minutiae of life. Choosing a random time and place in our past to pop into and observe how people from all social strata and cultures lived. Human history was littered with beautiful moments intertwined with tragic ones. I wish it had occurred to me then to count the number of smiles I'd seen, laughs I'd heard, tears I'd wanted to wipe away. Of course, no amount of data could fully capture the lived commonality between an Incan child in 5th century Peru and that of a Russian child in 22nd century Siberia. Those similarities could only be experienced in those times, with those people, and the memories later brought together to compare and contrast and always find, no matter what, that they shared so much more than they didn't.

I lingered on this thought as I waited for my consciousness to be sent into the universe, untethered, to arrive at its new destination as an omnipotent observer. It had to have been nearly ten minutes since I had entered CHAUCER. Something was wrong. I moved toward the door, calibrating the level of irritation to use in my voice when I asked Neil and Bill what the *fuck* they were doing. But the door was no longer where it should have been.

I realized that I had been floating in a dense black for a long while. No light, no sound, nothing that my senses could pick up on. I imagined, had my body traveled with my consciousness, the only thing I might feel would be an unbearable cold.

This was interesting, but predictable. The end of everything, we had always assumed, would be "The Great Rip." As far back as the 20th century we understood that the universe was expanding at an increasingly accelerated rate. Eventually atoms would tear apart and there would be nothing left of the universe except a cold, silent nothing.

I sent my consciousness away, searching for any remnants of the universe as I recognized it. Some remnant of humanity to prove our mastery over our fates. As I flit from place to place (for lack of a better word) and continually found more nothing, I realized my sense of time and place was gone. Fear, being a primarily physical sensation, is difficult to feel when traveling. In fact, until the moment I lost my sense of self in this unending void, I thought it impossible to feel. What need for fear does a wisp of consciousness have?

Still, it crept up on me. I again remembered all those moments lost to history. The people and their stories, their connections, no longer existed. No art survived. No buildings.

No religion. Not even memory was strong enough to survive the universe tearing itself into its constituent parts. All we fought and struggled to build was pointless.

A wave of nostalgia and melancholy washed over me. I sped up my search. In a place where time and space no longer existed I was able to explore and reexplore it all instantaneously.

There was nothing.

I searched again, looked for folds in space-time that might show me an alternate universe where what we did mattered. Where something tangible lasted.

How many times did I search in the time I was in the machine? An infinite number of times.

There was nothing.

Perhaps that's what tipped Dr. Orson over to insanity. He had called himself "enlightened" in our conversation. I suspected that, like me, he had realized the pointlessness of it all. Given enough time, when we finally reached the end of everything, all the things that made humanity special were for naught. Including any greater purpose we believed for ourselves.

As the realization of our ultimate fate settled into my core, the universe looked at me. Within the deep void a tear opened, wider and wider, until it filled my field of vision. An eye (for lack of a better descriptor) stared at me, unknowingly massive, and unimaginably old. I'm not sure how I know this, but I do.

Surrounding the ink-blot pupil was a roiling mist, and within that mist was the entirety of existence. I saw entire galaxies birthed and then die. Within those galaxies planets formed, lifeforms sprouted, and then it was all wiped out in a blink.

Voices called to me from the mist swirling in this creature's eye—voices I recognized. All of humanity called out to me to turn back, to forget them, to let them exist in their moment in peace, as it's all they'd ever have. I heard myself speaking with Dr. Orson.

Fear overtook my consciousness. A deep, existential dread. Meaninglessness and an overwhelming smallness swirled into a cocktail of panic. If I had the means to scream, I may have never stopped.

The eye's focus shifted past me. My novelty was no longer amusing, or perhaps I was never its interest to begin with, and the eye closed, leaving me alone in the void.

I sat there in the cold, silent nothing, and wished to go back to before all this. To never have to think of it again. To forget that the end was coming and there was nothing that anyone could do to stop it. No science or technology or religion or magic powerful enough to ward it off. In the end, there was nothing.

***

A sliver of light appeared in front of me. Like the great eye, it gradually widened until CHAUCER was filled with the white laboratory light. I shielded my eyes as a sense of my body returned to me. I was curled into the fetal position on the floor of CHAUCER, a long string of drool clinging to my chin. Neil and Bill grimaced as the smell of my emptied bowels hit them. I didn't care. These small embarrassments no longer mattered. Nothing did.

Like Dr. Orson, I found myself unable to speak of what I had seen for months afterward. The words escaped me. More than that, speaking felt meaningless. Everything felt meaningless.

I wouldn't even have written this were it not for your insistence on making the same mistake that Dr. Orson and myself have made. There is nothing to be gained by traveling to the end of everything. What you see as the ultimate knowledge is really nothing more than context for what we already know—existence is fleeting and meaningless. If there is a lesson in that, it's to allow the sun to grace your face while it's there. To hold the hand of the person you love more often. To find an individual purpose because there is no greater one.

My only hope is that this letter finds you in time. Regardless of your decision, Godspeed.

***

Eventually, everything will end. No matter what we as a species do, the universe is going to tear itself apart molecule by molecule. So, what comes after that? Will there be any remnant at all of what came before? What if we could find out?

When I was in high school and college I read a lot of 19th and early 20th century horror that revolved around scientists of other learned men coming up against things that no one can possibly understand. H.P. Lovecraft, Edgar Allan Poe, Nathaniel Hawthorne. Those types of writers and those types of stories that explored the limits of humanity's understanding and what happens when we cross over into territory our minds are incapable of processing. I hoped to capture some of that essence, here, in my own way.

EVERY DAY THE SAME DREAM

I woke up again today. Not one-hundred percent sure I wanted to. Still, I'm here, living the dream.

In this dream, my life is a series of buttons to be pushed. It starts with the alarm. Continues with the microwave, where I heat up my breakfast burrito. There is a button that locks my house with a *bzzz* and a *click*. A button that unlocks my car doors. Plays the car radio. Calls the elevator at the office. Every single key on my keyboard is a button (ones that make annoying *clickety-clackity* sounds—but buttons nonetheless). Buttons on a different microwave. Back to the elevator. Back to the car radio. Back to the lock. Over to the TV remote. I like those buttons best. They're colorful.

The details of my dream differ. Sometimes traffic is worse. Sometimes it's Karen's birthday. The broad strokes of it, the pieces I remember most clearly, never change.

A couple of days ago, I wondered if I could change any part of my dream. I wondered what control I actually have.

Instead of leaving through the front door of my house, I left through the back, stepping into the yard. Apparently, the sun rises in that direction and hangs there for a few hours. It was so bright I had to shield my eyes with my hands. In the corner of my yard a cardinal had built a nest on a branch of the tree, arranging twigs into a bowl. Pretty low branch. I hope no cats find it.

The change felt good. Even the air seemed somehow different from the front yard at this time of morning. Warmer. Sweeter. I cut around the side of the house. It was cooler in the house's shade. Just a little bit, but noticeable. But then I was at my car, pressing the button to unlock the doors. Pressing the buttons to change the radio station.

I slid back into my dream. Buttons and Karen's birthday and more buttons. By the time I got home I forgot to re-enter through the back door. Feels like I might have missed something. Maybe the cardinal's nest was finished. Or maybe it was gone, eaten by the cat I had tried to wish away. I should've checked, but it was late and I had to be up for work in the morning.

Yesterday, the night having successfully drained my brain of its exhaustion and cynicism for a few hours, I again resolved to try something new. To build on what I had started.

After my shower I stepped into the kitchen, the search for an opportunity to change fresh in my mind. My stomach gurgled with hunger and I instinctively went to the freezer (in as much as pulling food from a freezer can be considered instinct) but stopped short of the breakfast burritos. No part of me wanted to tap those microwave buttons.

Instead, I lowered myself to the fridge. There were eggs. I had green onions. Cheese. Everything I needed to make an omelet. It might make me late, as my morning routine was calibrated to maximize sleep, which meant variations from the norm would delay my commute to work, but this felt important.

I'm a poor cook, so the omelet was overdone. Still, it was better than another consecutive day of frozen breakfast burrito. Content, I slid the dishes into the dishwasher and washed the frying pan. Like the day before, I left through the back door. The cardinal's nest was there, but the cardinal was missing. Gone to collect more building materials, perhaps? I imagined the cardinal at some avian Home Depot, and smiled at the absurdity of it.

Again, like being placed on a conveyor belt, the rest of the day became the same dream. Except now I was aware of it. Prepared for it. I varied my routines at work. Instead of microwaving leftovers for lunch, I took a walk to a nearby restaurant and ate there. I tried to look out the window more. Karen noticed. "Are you okay?" she asked.

"Yes. Why?"

"You seem distracted."

I smiled. She had posited an interesting interpretation of my expression. Like she couldn't recognize engagement with the world outside of my computer screen and desk. She had to find other words.

"No," I said. "Just daydreaming a bit."

She nodded slowly, like she had the sudden realization that she was in conversation with a madman. That's fine. My dream isn't for her, anyway.

On the drive home I tried to think of other ways to break my routines. As I neared my street I was overcome with a desire to keep driving. I didn't want to be home, where I knew I'd make dinner and then fall into a trance in front of the TV, only to break from it the following morning. Time had an urgency to it, now. How much of it had I wasted without a thought in my head? How much of it had I spent waiting listlessly for the next day to arrive so I could move meaninglessly through it?

So I kept going. I drove aimlessly, turning down random residential streets, following their curves into one another like a series of tributaries that may or may not lead me to the ocean. Most houses were quiet, the lights from the televisions in their living rooms like private fireworks. Bursting into bright colors, all empty noise and harmless heat. I'm one of those people. If you had looked in on me just the night before there would be a similar strobe coming from my living room.

There were a few streets with people out. Children playing on front lawns, their parents standing guard nearby. Older people reading on their porches or just sitting, allowing the evening breeze to touch their face. I felt envious of them.

That night, after I had eaten dinner and people-watched at a small nearby diner, I sat on my porch. The night was cool and the chill wormed its way into my bones. But I stayed. And I was better for it.

This morning felt different. Like there was an urgency to sever the ties to my old routine in favor of a new one. A better one. I woke up before my alarm, showered, and made myself pancakes. I left through the backdoor—the cardinal was in its nest, sitting quietly, vigilant for threats—and walked around the house to my car. My finger hovered over the "unlock" button and I paused, suddenly aware that this is precisely the spot every morning where I fall into my dream. I'm only ever able to escape it when free from the car.

I turned away and walked. I had a vague idea of how to get to work by foot, but that would take hours. Instead, I went to the bus stop. There were others there—an old lady with a little metal grocery bin, some young kids wearing headphones—that stared at me like I was an alien come to observe their ways. I smiled as politely as I could, probably just as reassuring as an alien would be.

I had no idea what to do to get on the bus. Did it still take coins? Everyone seemed to have a card they swiped. Luckily, the bus driver allowed me on without one, taking the buck-fifty in cash but admonishing me to get a card for next time.

No longer forced to focus on the road, or curse at the other cars blocking my path, my mind wandered. Connections I'd have never made formed easily, problems that I'd struggled with for months suddenly solved with minimal effort. A clarity washed over me. Not of anything specific. Just of my being. I know it sounds crazy that something as simple as taking the bus unlocked this new potential in me, and it is, but I finally felt free of my daily dream and that was enough.

Or was it? Would my dream just start later once I got to the office? When I was sitting at my cubicle, Karen yammering away on her phone in the cube next to me, would that sense of sameness return?

A salvation appeared in the window in front of me. I pulled the chime and the bus stopped at the next designated corner. I had to backtrack a few blocks, but when I arrived I knew this was where I wanted to be.

I called into work, claiming to be sick. No questions were asked, just a half-hearted "feel better" uttered from the other end of the phone. I wasn't sure what I expected. I'm not an important cog in that machine, as much as I like to pretend I am.

I entered through the gates and took a deep breath. The air was sweet with pollen and grass clippings. A bumble bee buzzed by me. It felt good to be outside, bucking my traditional day, even though I knew it wouldn't last. It didn't need to. A single day every once in a while is enough to make the rest of the slog tolerable. At least, I hope that's true.

Every tombstone in the cemetery has a story to tell. The love between the family buried together. The tragedy of the child that died too soon. One day my story will rest in a place like this, and I wonder what sort of story it will be.

That's not giving myself enough credit. My story is what I make it. Every day should be a new dream.

***

A few years ago I stumbled on a browser-based game called **Every day the same dream**[1]. *It's a short game—should only take you 15 minutes to play the entire thing, should you wish to do that—but impactful. It's about a white-collar worker stuck in a rut. The premise of the game is simple: Every day you follow simple clues that lead you to experience one new thing that breaks your routine a bit, until the ultimate routine-breaking act.*

Considering the game was made in six days, it's expertly crafted. It wraps up a lot of the existential dread (or boredom, more accurately) I, and I think many others, feel day-to-day while providing a sense of catharsis. I wanted to pay tribute to that. Use the game as a way to verbalize my thoughts about being white-collar and living comfortably but passionless. That said, I wanted to do it in a more optimistic way than the game.

That's where the idea sprung from. A combination of my own thoughts and feelings about my life, made digital by this game. Where I changed course from the game is in my approach to the message. Life often feels like its not in your control, and in many ways it may not be, but there are certain things we can do to engage with the world around us. Change our routine a little bit. Eat healthier. Find new perspectives on the things we interact with every day, like leaving from the back door of your house instead of the front. Taking a second to notice a cardinal building a nest. All of it is meaningful if you choose to search for that meaning.

I hope the story isn't too navel-gazing. It's a privilege to be who I am, with the job I have, and the existential panic I sometimes deal with makes that easy to forget. Taking control of the small things, inserting minor changes in the day-to-day, can help to keep that in perspective.

---

[1] *https://www.molleindustria.org/everydaythesamedream/everydaythesamedream.html*

SAY SOMETHING NEW

Pour the ink down your throat
Spit words onto the page
Pull them from deep in your gut

Soak your hands in the ink and bile
Swirl the concoction
Look at what you've done
What's been created

Something new? No.
Something unique? Also no.

But something with feeling

And as the ink dries
On paper,
In mouth,
You'll have connected to something
More than yourself

Maybe that's enough

Maybe that's all there is

***

The wonderful and horrifying thing about the human experience is that everyone's experience is unique, but also shared. We all experience the same types of things filtered through the sum total of our other experiences and the specific circumstances in which we live. Because of this, as a writer there is nothing that I can say that hasn't already been said (probably better) and no idea I can explore that hasn't already been explored. What can be done is to explore those ideas through the specific lens in which I live.

Still, pulling those words from wherever they come from is tough. It's work. So, sometimes I can't help but wonder what I'm doing it for, if everything's been said better than I can say it. The only conclusion I can draw that keeps me going is that it doesn't matter. What matters is how art connects you to something bigger than yourself. In that sense, it's all worthwhile.

DISTANCE

My fingers drifted over her palm, a microscopic yet infinite space between, and somehow felt the softness of her skin.

"Clone THX-1988. What do you think?" Dr. Abello asked. Her curiosity was sincere, if clinical.

"Amber," I corrected. Then sighed. "I know it's not her." I searched the young woman's eyes for memories I knew we didn't share.

"You'll always know it's not her—not on an intellectual or emotional level," she said. "But this is the closest you'll ever get. We've finely gotten to one-hundred percent genetic similarity."

She was right. I knew that. Her face was like Amber's. The overbite. The beauty mark on her forehead. Even the shade of her skin was perfect. I still knew it wasn't her. Not really.

"This is it," Dr. Abello said. "Our last attempt."

The bay door boomed and bent and creaked and cracked under the assault on its other side. They would soon be inside, angry at how I'd wasted the resources meant to keep them alive. I didn't care.

I turned away and gazed out at the rows of tubes holding other Ambers, each less perfect than this one. Each less perfect than my Amber. The Amber I left behind.

"I'm sorry I let it get this far. We should have known better. You've been a good friend to me."

"I didn't do this for you," Dr. Abello clarified. "I've been sending my research back to Earth since we began." Then, as an afterthought, "What do we do with them all?"

There was no good answer. I walked away from her knowing that the generation ship took me 22 miles further from Amber every second. 79,200 miles further from her every hour. 1,900,800 miles further from her every day.

I walked away knowing that no matter how many pictures I kept of her, how many memories I relived, nor how many clones I sanctioned in the hopes of cauterizing my self-inflicted wound—I would never see her again. In all likelihood she was already dead, the effects of relativity cruelly allowing her to live out her remaining years in a fraction of my own. It was pointless.

I stopped and Dr. Abello straightened. "I'm opening the bay doors," I said. "We'll let them decide what happens next."

***

I'm fascinated by relative distance. You and I have a specific perspective based on our size. To every person, a pebble is small and a mountain is almost unfathomably big. But to a mite (that may or may not live in your eyelashes), the pebble is unfathomably big and the mountain is beyond comprehension.

Because of our size relative to them, we can't even see mites. And to them, we're an entire world on which to live, explore, and die.

It's these types of thoughts that inspired this story. I wanted to write something that explored this theme. What better way to illustrate that than by setting it on a spacecraft traveling at 1/10th the speed of light? The universe to us is like a mountain to a mite: beyond comprehension.

Still, there is no story without a human element. To deepen the theme, I also wanted to explore emotional distance. Someone who misses someone else enough to try to close the very real distance between them with science that they know can never be good enough to be authentic.

The first line illustrates this. Starting at the microscopic, where the atoms that make up one persons skin have the same amount of space between them as there is between stars, questions whether we can ever really be touching one another. Slowly the story pulls out until the we understand the distance between our protagonist and his lost love, Amber—1,900,800 miles everyday.

ERYN'S DREAM

She awoke next to her dream
On a bed of forget-me-nots

In the dream's voice she heard
The pleasant chime of a person's laughter
The instinctual panic of a child's scream
The confidence of an unfaithful lover's lie
She heard the sorrow
Of every parent who's lost a child
The bitterness
Of every brother and sister
That lost a sibling
She listened
To all of the emotions she would vocalize
And the ones she couldn't
Or wouldn't

In the dream's eyes she saw
The shards of a first crushes' broken heart
The wavering smile of a first love's disappointment
The wide eyes of a first-born's wonderment

She saw motivation on the face of a girl
Told she's not good enough
Nervousness on the face of a boy
Afraid of rejection
The crushed hopes and broken dreams
Of a son, daughter, father, mother, friend, lover
Who only wanted more
She saw the men she would love
And the inner-children she would hate
Every person that would love her
But she couldn't love back
She saw the people she loved
And wondered if they loved her

On her dream's breath she smelled
The foul waste of a person left alone
The acrid desperation of a woman falling apart
But trying to hold herself together
The flowery sweetness of a teenage boy's whisper
And the antiseptic bitterness of that whisper's intentions
She smelled the musk
Of two bodies entangled
As the whisper swayed her
And she smelled alcohol

On her dream's tongue she tasted
The salt of tears lost in a public bathroom
In some city, somewhere
The drugs taken to forget those tears
The sweat pouring
From the faces, arms, legs
Of children and their parents
Working to survive
She tasted iron blood lost in the street

<u>THROUGH DARK INTO LIGHT</u>

For the sin of being a different shade of human
Blood lost on the battlefield
For the sin of being young
Blood lost in the bedroom
For the sin of holding onto innocence

In her dream's touch she felt
The goosebumps of a nightmare
Or fantasy realized
The shaking guilt of a wrong
The tightened fist
Of a woman wronged
She felt every bruised, broken, bleeding wrist
Of someone who gave up on nothing but themselves
The sting of a missed opportunity
Or a missed friend

She felt herself falling
Into self-actualization
Self-awareness
Self-realization
Selflessness

***

I wrote this poem in my early twenties for one of my best friends. I don't recall if it was for any special occasion (maybe her birthday?) but it turned out differently than I had intended, and doesn't reflect her personality particularly well. What interests me about this poem now, and the reason why I included it in this collection, is because of its empathy. For some reason I can't recall some 15 years onward, Eryn inspired empathy in me. Whatever the poem's technical flaws, or clumsy wording, or lack of focus, it's bursting with empathy. That's an important thing.

THOUGHTS AND ACTIONS IN A CAR CRASH

The ice is unexpected, though it shouldn't be. Temperatures have been below freezing for days, a constant dusting of snow either falling or blowing onto the roads to mask the slickness beneath.

Bumper-to-bumper traffic during rush hour is expected. Mundane, even.

It's this combination of expectations that leads to the crash.

Not checking the phone for a text might have been the variable that negated at least one circumstance. Instead, the phone was the distraction that closed the margin of error for the expected enough that the unexpected became a major factor in events.

Shitshitshit.

The car jutters as the anti-lock brakes take hold, but doesn't slow.

Hands grip the steering wheel hard enough to leave marks. Eyes flutter to the side-view mirrors, hoping that the next lane is open to swerve.

It's not. Rush hour, after all.

Nonono.

Eyes wide, pupils dilated—observe each mistake in slow motion. As the distance closes the minivan becomes larger. Soon it's the entire field of view.

I'm sorry.

Impact. Everything thrown forward. Seatbelt locks, stealing breath. Head off steering wheel. No airbag. Blood.

When the flash of white dissipates there are voices. "Are you okay?" "I saw what happened. Shouldn't tailgate in this weather." "Damn phones should be illegal on the road."

For once, the assigned blame is accurate.

Stupid.

Open the door, face the victim. There are children crying. Their mother doing her best to calm them. Assure them enough that they'll eventually feel safe in the van again. Her eyes show no anger or blame, thankfully. Instead, they're full of anxiety. A bit of relief that it wasn't worse.

"I'm sorry. It was my fault."

She nods, unable to speak with the adrenaline making her shake.

Turn away. Wait for the police. Other cars are leaning on their horns, now. Wasn't just her day that's fucked. Made a bad situation worse.

Damn.

***

I originally wrote this story in college as a mess of bolded text, italics, and parentheticals in an attempt to capture how our thought processes overlap, speed up, get distracted, slow down, etc. It wasn't an easy read.

But I loved the idea. So I rewrote it from scratch in an attempt to simplify it. I focused only on what the title allowed—thoughts and actions—and did away with the rest. I think it's an interesting way to capture a hyper-specific moment in time.

ODE TO THE ELLIPSES

Dot. Dot. Dot.
All he can think to write.
Dot. Dot. Dot.

To represent a pause.
A pained thought.
A symbol of silence.

For a millisecond.
For an eternity.

Three pools of ink, infinitely deep,
To be all the things we don't dare say.

***

Ernest Hemingway wrote about striving to write "one true sentence" to get his workday started each morning. Often, when I think about doing that for myself, I see a Sunday comics-style word bubble appear above my head, three ellipses blinking within. That sounds like a problem, but as the poem states ellipses can be a wonderful thing. As punctuation, as emphasis, as

*pause for effect—they're versatile. So this is my way of showing
appreciation to an under-appreciated punctuation. Thank you, ellipses, for
all that you do.*

LETTER(S) TO THE GIRL(S) I (ONCE) LOVE(D)

There was a letter written to someone, somewhere, once. It may have read, in part:

"Dear [REDACTED],

A cold wind pushed us apart, but I'm hoping the convection currents will heat us again. I can live in this cycle for the rest of my life, happily, as long as it's with you. You love my hobbies but sometimes forget they aren't me. That's okay, though. I understand it and, if that's the only way you'll love me, I accept it.

Do you remember the first time we held hands? The first time we kissed? Made love? I think I do, but it all seems like such a far-away dream at this point. Mountains rising from buildings, and people trimming clouds in their front yard. Beautiful, but nonsensical.

When you said goodbye to me in that parking lot I knew it would be the last time. I tried to savor the moment—I took still photographs of your hair, eyes, lips, and smile; I recorded your voice and laugh; I wrote poetry about your movements—

all in the hopes that those final few fleeting moments could somehow be immortal.

Of course, they weren't. How could they be? Even then we were changing. As much as I wanted to steal the sand from our hourglass to hide in my heart, the grains were too small. They slid right through my fingers and kept falling. I realized then that my memory was all I would have to rely on. It's a shame memory is so fallible.

Eventually my memory of you degraded into dream, and from dream into fantasy, and from fantasy into ideal. My memory of you became almost political, or religious. Remember when we rode bikes to that beautiful church by my apartment? Me neither.

The point is: I was never mad.

I know you probably thought I was, and I probably let you believe it. But I wasn't. You know this already, but it can be hard to understand the future.

Because I saw it, sweetheart, and I didn't like it. Of all the possible futures that could have been mine, the one without you in it was the one I wanted to avoid. Yet, in my avoidance I'm the one that brought it to fruition. When it started to come true I panicked. In my mind there was no other option. I was scrambling to find a solution that was never there.

[REDACTED], you've made me want to burn every piece of paper you've inspired me to write. Destroy every happy ending I wish we could have had. And yet, if this were one of my stories you love so much I would have found the solution and our hands would be interlocked as we sleep once again. Unfortunately, this isn't a story, and a solution doesn't exist. I just wanted to let you know I haven't stopped looking and I never will. Hopefully, one day I'll be able to make you understand why."

And someone, somewhere, never read that letter.

***

This is an old story. I don't mean that in the metaphorical sense, as in this is a boy-loses-girl story as old as time, although it is that. I mean I wrote the original version of this shortly after college, while coming to terms with a break-up.

It's changed since then. I've revised the story to be more playful with language, more bold in its metaphors, more focused in its theme, but its origin is that of a heartsick young man that felt like he had sabotaged himself.

With those ingredients I intended the story to explore memory—how it can change over time, how it differs from person to person. We rarely appreciate the things we have in the moment, so we're forced to rely on our imperfect memories. There's a lot of sadness in that perspective. How can we ever truly appreciate what we have if our only experiences of it are in hindsight, when it's been filtered into something different?

The story also touches on inadvertently making fears real. By loving someone too hard, too fast, and thereby being afraid of losing them, you can push them away. It's cautionary in that sense.

There is a lot going on--perhaps too much. It's not quite focused. A little messy. But I like that about it. I think it's an accurate reflection of relationships and, especially, those feelings after a break-up, no matter how amicable.

A BRIEF HISTORY OF THEIR LOVE

They met in "Psychology 302: Elements of Consciousness" during their junior year of college. Both were taking it as a general requirement, and both would later explain that they had chosen this particular course to better understand their own inner-workings. He was 21 years old. She was an android.

She kept it from him, at first. Androids had integrated into society years before he was born, and the ones lucky enough to be built as perfect simulacrums of humans kept it a secret for fear of discrimination—although the secrets never helped to build trust. She waited over a year, adjusting her behaviors to match his expectations. She ate like a person, claiming to be picky about food when confronted with things that might harm her. Each night her best friend, another android, helped her to clean out the array that comprised her body systems.

When there were enough rumors surrounding her and their relationship that it seemed inevitable he would find out, she asked him to take a walk with her. There wasn't much explanation needed. She simply told him and watched for the micro-expressions that would reveal his true feelings. To her surprise, there were none. Instead, he asked if she cared about him. She told him she did. "Then we'll be fine," he said, taking her hand in his. She liked that he was casual about it. She wanted to know what it felt like to be loved. She wondered if she could know what it felt like to give love.

Together, they found it possible. She struggled to describe her feelings, wishing she had her own vocabulary to account for the differences in physiology and emotional capability, but all androids relied on human vernacular to communicate. Like a script, there were things she knew he wanted to hear. Things that would accomplish her objective of keeping him near. Things like her insistence that he made her 'feel' different; that she 'missed' him when he was gone; that he made her 'happy'. For his part, he never gave it much thought. "Consciousness is consciousness," he said, "And I love yours." She wasn't as sure about his conclusions, but his strength gave her strength.

Most people didn't see it that way. His family balked when he introduced her. His mother cried and wondered how they would have children. His father reminded him that there was a time when androids were humanity's greatest enemies. That his grandfather had died fighting that war. His friends mocked him mercilessly. Asked what she felt like on the inside. If she was cold or if he had to use oil and grease to slide inside of her. If his ejaculate bound up her gears. Telling him that androids were invented as sex toys and that he was partaking in a long and storied tradition of using an inanimate object when he couldn't otherwise get laid. He played along, absorbed their prejudice with his own good humor and self-deprecation. He told them that he didn't have to worry about getting her pregnant. That she was durable. They became serious and asked how he could trust anything about her. Her emotions, her body, her motivations—all manufactured. He explained that wasn't true, that he believed everything she said about their relationship, but in reality he preferred not to think about it.

Her family was non-existent. Her earliest memory was staring at a high, industrial ceiling, then being told to stand.

From then on she was on her own, every survival need pre-programmed into her. Her friends, other androids, couldn't understand the affection for the boy. They told her it was dangerous. That even if she weren't physically destroyed by people for encroaching on their biological imperative, she would be emotionally destroyed by this boy when he found flesh and blood that suited him better than her synthetic skin and computer brain. They reminded her that he will age and she will not. That he will die, and she will not. She preferred not to think about it.

The first attacks came not long after taking their relationship public. They were walking home from a movie when a group of his college friends drove by in a pickup and threw a Molotov cocktail at her. It shattered at her feet and she went up in flames. He threw himself on top of her, dampening the flames with his jacket and, fool that he was, with his body.

Weeks later, after she was reskinned, she visited him in the hospital. He marveled at her new skin. She studied his scars. The way his skin folded in on itself. The sheen it kept. "It's like nothing even happened," he told her as he ran his shaking fingers down her arm.

Touching his scars, she wondered how something so fragile survived in such a dangerous world.

The next year he proposed. Marriage between man and android was illegal, but he said it didn't matter since he didn't have to worry about her getting sick. "It's just a piece of paper and some legality," he said. "What's important is the vow. I vow to love you, forever." She smiled and thought that her forever was different than his. Still, despite that logic, there was something in her that didn't want to be without him. They said their vows in front of three androids beneath a full moon. To her surprise, she meant it when she told him there was nothing that could take her from him.

Because of the previous attacks, they fled to someplace no one knew them. When they moved in together she suggested that if someone figured out that she wasn't human and asked about it, they explain that she was a servant-android, kept to help him with the house. It was safer, she explained. He fought with her but she was unrelenting, and eventually he agreed. In private, they were like any other married couple. He went to sleep at 930, she pretended that she slept to be next to him. He woke up at 6am. She made his breakfast and prepared his lunch. He went to work. She busied herself around the house. He came home at 430. They ate dinner together in front of the television at 530. Every day.

Their neighbors realized she was synthetic within a few months. From then on, in public she acted as his assistant. This seemed to work. The violence didn't rise above the everyday discrimination androids always faced. She knew this bothered him, but he never spoke of it and she never pried. His physical safety was her main concern, even if she recognized that his emotional well-being may be compromised. They preferred not to think about it.

He retained his youth until his mid-thirties. Then his gut began to protrude, his hair thinned and lost its color, and his eyes sagged. "I'm sorry I can't stay as attractive as you," he said. "I'd understand if you wanted a younger guy." He meant it. She assured him that she loved him for his consciousness, and nothing else. He found that funny.

As he neared forty, his biological needs panicked. "I'm going to die without children," he said, "Without a family to carry on my lineage." She wondered why that was important. He told her he didn't expect her to understand. She was only an android, after all. She was silent, aware that he wanted to see her cry. She couldn't give him what he wanted, so she left the room. Less than an hour later he apologized.

When he became distant and spent more time away from home, she knew he was having an affair. She thought of the human language and her 'feelings.' Online forums said she should be 'jealous,' so that's what she ascribed to herself, although it wasn't accurate. There were no words to describe the unique combinations of electronic signals and synthesized hormones that coursed through her gelatin brain and allowed her to understand and interact with the world. She just knew that the connection she felt to him never wavered.

After a time, he admitted to it. "I'm sorry," he said. She told him it was alright, that she understood. "She's pregnant," he said. Still, she understood. His biological needs were important on an evolutionary scale. She couldn't compete with that. After all, it's only a body he needed. She would always have his consciousness. He smiled, but there were tears in his eyes.

He introduced her to his son and the other woman. The other woman looked at her, amused, and referred to her as the 'fuckbot.' She waited for him to defend her, to explain that her body was only a vessel for what she really offered him—a consciousness to share his life with. But no defense came. She wondered if the world wouldn't be easier without this other woman.

She resented having to pretend to be the family's servant-bot while they were out. The child and woman treated her as a toy, or a pet, or a maid. He still treated her fairly. But he no longer slept next to her, instead choosing to sleep with his biological imperative. Something strange happened within her circuits—some dull heat that she had never felt before. Still unable to ascribe a human word to it, she preferred to think of it as analogous to anger.

She watched as they slept. The scars on his chest and shoulders were reminders of his love for her. His willingness to sacrifice himself for her. They were reminders of how fragile human life is.

The woman didn't have the time or strength to struggle when her larynx was crushed. Her eyes went wide and she made a strange sound with the sharp intake of air—the last oxygen that would grace her lungs—but otherwise she was still. Next, she went to the child's room and repeated the process.

He didn't even wake until the next morning. When he did, she sat next to him, held his hand, and calmly explained what happened and why. He nodded, said he understood, and she watched his face for the micro-expressions that would tell her his true feelings.

He hid them well, but in his eyes there was something she had never seen before: Fear. She recognized the mistake she had made. Still, it was too late. The other woman was gone. So she gave him a choice to leave or stay. He asked for time.

Time passed, and he didn't bring it up. They achieved a sense of normalcy.

One day, she asked him if he missed his biological imperative. If she had acted in a way to change his feelings toward her. "I prefer not to think about it," he said.

The remainder of their lives were uneventful. He slept next to her. She was never able to explain what she felt.

He grew old. She never aged. When he died, she let go of her old life and began anew.

***

In music and spoken word there is a certain type of storytelling that I find beautiful but hard to describe. Songs like Terrible Things *by Mayday* Parade, *or* Don't Take the Girl *by Tim McGraw. Poetry from* Levi the Poet *or* Shane Koyczan. *Despite the differences in style and content, what these works have in common is the ability to tell powerful stories that span long periods of time and several events in a high-level, summarized, but still relatable way.*

When done right, I find that seeing the most important moments of a character's existence can be just as powerful as experiencing them in media res. But there is a trick to doing that right, I think. It has to do with the old writing advice "show, don't tell."

Generally, it's good advice. The curtain between the author and the reader is less transparent when the story is told in an immersive way, with characters acting things out in real time. That said, there is a tradition of "telling, not showing" that goes back centuries. Oral traditions, music, and poetry all "tell" in various ways. It's a viable, important, and powerful way to tell a story.

With this story, I wanted to show was the long arc of a relationship that society doesn't approve of. There are lots of stories about forbidden relationships, whether because of race, status, family feuds, or something else. Even human-synthetic relationships aren't new ground. Identifying those moments that were most important to a long-term relationship between man and machine was my spin, and what I was most interested in.

The challenge was choosing the right moments to summarize the pain, internal and external, of their relationship. When they met, how they fell in love, the trials they both faced in continuing forward despite all logic, the inevitabilities, and the denouement.

From a purely writing perspective, I needed to keep forward momentum and active language to hopefully make the reader forget they're reading what is essentially a summary of a full arc.

I like the story. I think it's an interesting snapshot of a unique relationship. It touches on themes of discrimination, language, biology, and the weird habit people have of ascribing feelings and emotions to inanimate things.

TO GO BACK

"What. Is. This?" Julie asked as she stepped into the garage, her suitcase dropping to the cement next to her.

Barry peered around his machine, confused as to why she was there. He glanced at the suitcase and remembered: she and her husband were visiting for the week with their son, Elijah. If he could still manage that type of flexibility, Barry would have kicked himself for forgetting. "Hey. Are you early?"

She stepped up to the machine, running her hand along its hard edges. The crow's feet extending from the corners of her eyes deepened with her furrowed brow. "No. I told you we were landing at 12:30. I thought maybe you'd want to pick us up from the airport."

"Oh. You know I don't like to drive, anymore. Reflexes aren't what they used to be." Barry stepped out from behind the machine, setting down the torque wrench he was using to tighten the final bolts. He unconsciously rubbed his liver-spotted hands together.

"Looks like you've been busy. That's why, right?" Julie asked, more than a little concern in her voice. Barry nodded. He certainly had been busy. The machine had consumed his thoughts for the weeks he'd been building it. "Are you going to explain this to me, or do I have to guess?"

"Where are Sam and Elijah?" he asked, peeking his head from the garage door into the connected house.

"Elijah was cranky from travel so Sam's laying him down for a nap."

"Oh. Okay." Barry took a seat at his workbench and looked for a long time at Julie, deciding how best to explain what he'd built. "What's the last moment you remember with your mother?"

She didn't even have to think about it. "Holding her hand as she passed."

"Ok, what's the last *good* moment you remember having with her? In person."

"That was a good moment."

"Sorry. Last *normal* moment, maybe."

This, Julie had to consider. "Two Christmases ago. We were washing dishes after dinner, just the two of us, and she talked about how proud she was of me. Told me stories about what it was like watching me grow up. Said she sees a lot of me in Elijah."

"How did you feel in that moment? Do you remember?"

"I was content, I guess. Thought it was weird she was so nostalgic, but that's what the holidays do to people. And, I guess, she knew she was losing her memories. Probably wanted to reflect before she couldn't, anymore." Julie sighed, trying to appreciate the beauty of remembering but only finding the pain of it. "To be honest I was distracted, thinking about the plane ride home. I was nervous because Sam and Elijah are both so anxious about flying. I'm sorry, Dad, but I'm not sure what any of this has to do with—" she gestured to the machine in the middle of the garage.

"It's a time machine," Barry stated.

Julie laughed. "A time machine?" Barry nodded. "What for? To go back in time and prevent Mom from getting Alzheimer's?"

"C'mon, Julie. Don't be mean. I know there isn't anything I can do to prevent what happened. That's not what it's for."

Julie leaned against the workbench to be closer to Barry. "I'm not trying to be mean. I just… well, I don't understand."

"If you could go back to relive that Christmas, but instead of thinking about the flight and Sam and Elijah you understood that those were the last moments you'd have with Mom when she was clear, would you do it?"

"Of course."

"When you get to be my age you start to think back on things. Remember all those last moments you didn't know would be the last ones. The last time I got to play poker with all the guys, before we went our separate ways. The last time I spoke to my brother, before his addiction. And the last time I got to hold your mother before she lost herself. This is a way for me to do that."

"To change things? Dad…"

He waved the suggestion away. "No. Nothing like that. What's to change? If I changed even the smallest thing I might not be here now, with you, and with Sam and Elijah just upstairs. Despite the disappointments and heartbreak, I'd never risk being where I am now, with you. I just want to go back to live in those other moments for a little longer. To appreciate them a little bit more. We don't know when our last moments with anyone might be, so how can we fully appreciate them?"

Julie placed her hand on Barry's shoulder. "It's a good idea, Dad. A great one." Barry took her hand in his own. "But before you go, can you live in the moment with us for a little while?"

Barry smiled. "There isn't anything I want more."

Together, they left the machine in the garage and went upstairs to say hello to Sam and Elijah.

***

When I was barely into my 20s I went on a bike ride with my best friends. It was something we hadn't done in a long time, having graduated from bikes to our own cars years before. We rode around our old neighborhood, then expanded into other neighborhoods nearby. I remember the day clearly, not least of all because I had a nagging thought throughout that this adventure might be one of the last times the three of us would do something like that.

These feelings got me thinking about appreciation. About how, impossible it is (at least, without the benefit of hindsight) to fully appreciate the moment you're in or the people you're with. We're not built to have that perspective. But what if there was a way?

Time travel has always fascinated me. In a sense, time travel is the ultimate form of control. If you make a mistake but have access to a time machine, that mistake can be corrected. And if you remember the last moments you had with someone, you can relive it to better appreciate it at the time.

Both of these concepts—nostalgia and time travel—are core concepts in some of Ray Bradbury's work. You may sense some of his influence in the story. I don't try to ape his style (anymore), but for this story I wanted to hit the same tone and tackle similar themes that he might. Use some of the same language. Especially for Barry. He strikes me as a Bradbury-type character.

Most of all, I hope that this story makes you consider being a bit more present. Live in the moments you have with the ones you love with no distraction.

SMALL DECISIONS

Mistakes are made in small moments. Consequences are felt in big ones.

This is where I find myself now, lying in bed with the consequences sliding down my cheeks. You don't know yet. I don't want to tell you. I don't know how to tell you, or what to tell you. I tell myself that my penance can be my guilt slowly eating my insides until I'm nothing but a hollow husk. My punishment can be the knowledge that I broke the only promise you've ever asked me to keep. I know, though, that those are only easy ways to make me feel less selfish about a selfish act. And none are fair to you.

You'll ask why. Why did I do it? Because I wanted to see if I could get away with it. Because I was drunk. Because you made me mad a few weeks ago. Because I like the attention. Because I knew she wanted it, and who am I to disappoint? Because I have low self-esteem. Because it's a mixture of all these things and none of them.

Does it really matter when you're crying because of my mistake?

Maybe that's the punishment I deserve. To face my shame. Watch you float away from me and know that I'm the one who gave the push. I love you too much to hide. To lie.

And it is bad. You fall to your knees in tears. I walk away, come back, walk away again. I beg you to hit me, but you can't bring yourself to touch me at all. I fall to the ground next to you. I beg, I apologize, I cry harder than you are. I look around the room at all of our things, our pictures, our paintings, our books, *our our our.* We built a life together and with a yes-or-no decision I demolished it all. Because my weakness was greater than my love for a brief, important moment.

You tell me you trusted me. I know. You tell me that I was supposed to be different than the others. I know. You tell me this is the worst hurt you've ever felt.

I know.

We discuss next steps. You want to sleep in the other room, but that's not fair. I'll go. No, you say, the pillows smell like you and it makes me want to throw up. I understand.

You tell me you thought I loved you. I do love you, now more than ever. I explain that now that I've done something so stupid, so utterly and irrevocably unforgivable, it's clear to me how much I love you. I say, more to myself than to you, that it's a shame that we need to hurt people so badly to see how much they mean to us. I say that I know I love you because I don't love her, if that makes any sense.

Then, in a fit of cosmic justice, you make a small decision with a big consequence.

You forgive me.

***

Early in my relationship with my now wife, I made a mistake. A big one. One that could have—perhaps should have, if you're a certain type of person—ended our relationship. Snuffed out the potential that we've only just realized with our marriage, our house, and our child, years after the fact.

This story tries to capture those feelings one wrestles with after a mistake that hurts the person you love. The guilt, panic, shame, and regret. The anger with oneself. The sobering reality that relationships take a long time to build but can end in seconds.

Luckily for me, my wife forgave me then. She showed me that an act of selfishness can be balanced with one of selflessness. She allowed us to build the life we have now and for that I'll be forever grateful.

YOU WILL BE REMEMBERED

I will remember you
Daily, weekly, monthly
Your name crawling
From the depths of my mind
The key that unlocks my secrets

I will remember you
Because you are the answer
To my security question
When I forget my password

I wish there were other options
Than "Who was your first girlfriend?"
I could lie
And begin to forget

But then I wouldn't remember you.

***

Because I'm security-conscious (paranoid?) I've set-up the majority of my logins to need multi-factor authentication. Sometimes this takes the form of additional security questions that rotate through my history. You've seen them: What was the name of your first pet? What street did you grow up on? What is the name of your favorite teacher in high school? What is your mother's maiden name? Etc., etc.

Aside from being easy to uncover by clever scammers (seriously, if a stranger starts asking you personal questions that hit on any of those topics, don't answer them), it occurred to me that these may also be negative reminders of people whose names might conjure deeper emotions than nostalgia. Whether good or bad I don't know, that depends on you, but I'm at a point in my life where it's kind of funny. So, this poem is my attempt at capturing those strange feelings.

HER TEA

Every night Cassie made tea and read until her eyelids slowly shut, sleep whisking her away. Not always the same tea. No, she varied her tastes. Green tea, chamomile, mint, ginger, mixed berry—on any given night her tastes were guided by something I'm not sure even she understood.

Once a month we went to a boutique tea and spice shop in Old Town. She browsed for what felt like hours, opening each container of tea and taking long, sumptuous sniffs of the leaves inside. I didn't mind. Seeing her happy made me happy, and the place was fun to explore. Once in a while I'd even find a good spice rub for grilling steaks. When she'd had her fill on samples (or maybe when her sense of smell was dulled to oblivion) she would pick out three or four packets of tea, and we'd go home. She would make whatever struck her fancy that night, then sit and read until the pot was gone.

She did this every night. And every morning I would find her teacup in the living room, where she did her reading, only a small puddle of cold tea soaking a spattering of leaves left at the cup's bottom. So, every morning I would take the cup to the kitchen and wash it before making breakfast and getting ready for work.

The first few times this happened, she thanked me. Promised to do better. But after a little while—a few days or a few weeks, I don't remember—it became expectation. Part of our routine was her drinking tea and reading late into the night, and me getting up early and cleaning it. I think this may have bothered some people, but not me. I found it endearing. She probably noticed without ever saying anything, but one of my favorite things to do before bed was to peek in on her curled up with a cup of tea and a book in the little egg chair we kept in the corner (she called it her "book nook"), the fragrance of the tea wafting throughout our tiny apartment, and her content to be somewhere else for a little while.

For her, it was an escape. Our routine was for me, too, considering the difficulties we faced in the daytime. I was at the beginning of my career, barely making $45k to work 60-hour weeks. She was in medical school, accruing more debt in six months than I earned in a year. We were far from home, alone in an expensive new city. And she had to deal with all the guilt of someone who left behind a sick mother. Those few hours per night were the closest either of us came to calm. A recurring eye of a storm that washed over us anew with daybreak.

Her tea was the warning. One night I peeked in on her and she had her book, but her tea was untouched. She only stared ahead. "You okay?" I asked.

She snapped out of her reverie. "Yeah. Going to bed?"

I didn't think much of it at the time. Cass had just gotten word from her sister that their mother had taken a turn. Instead of her cancer going into remission, it had spread. The medical bills were piling up. She was too young for Medicare and her health insurance was quickly meeting its maximums. Of course she'd be distracted. Thoughtful. Worried.

On another night, I don't remember when exactly, she asked me for advice while she brewed her nightly pot. "Should I take time off?" she asked. "I feel like I should go home."

"I don't know," I answered, somewhere between truth and lie. If every answer could be mapped on a spectrum from right to wrong, my feelings were firmly in the middle. I could see the guilt eating away at her, the fact that she wasn't with her mother in what looked to be her final days weighing on her, but if she went home then she wouldn't be with me. Either way, there was time someone would never be able to get back. "Will it affect school?"

She shrugged. "Yeah. I'll graduate later."

"Will it affect your loans?"

"I'll have to start paying them off before graduation."

"Oh."

"Yeah. Not ideal."

She carried the teapot into the living room, lit the tea candle inside the warming stand, and gently placed the pot on top. With that, she picked up her book and allowed herself to disappear for the night. Not wanting to bother her, I went to bed, but couldn't sleep. Eventually, she joined me. We both lay awake all night, holding hands.

The semester ended. My job had gotten more demanding. On most days, I'd leave before Cass was awake and return as she was nearing the end of her tea pot. Exhausted, I might grab a snack and a shower before crawling into bed, dreading the Sisyphean task of doing it all over again the next day.

In hindsight, perhaps it was my own absence that led to hers. I came home from work late one night and the apartment smelled empty. There was no fragrance of jasmine, or chamomile, or berry. No flickering light spilling out into the hallway. And no Cass.

Too tired to panic, I called her cell phone.

"Hey," she answered.

"Hey. Where are you?"

"Home."

"How is she?"

"Sick. Getting worse. Hopefully there's some time left."

"I'm sorry," I said, hoping that I could somehow imbue the words with the layers of meaning I needed to express and she needed to hear. "How long will you be gone?"

"I don't know. I think I need to stay with her. I've already lost a lot of time."

"I understand."

We were both quiet. An unasked but perhaps already answered question hung over everything we might say. "Tell your mom I send my love," I said.

"I will. Good night."

She hung up. Still, I kept the phone to my ear. Listening for the ghost of her voice to ask me to join her, even if it meant risking our livelihood. To make up for the time we lost in our own problems, our own worlds, even though we were supposed to be inextricably tied together in every way. Listening for her to tell me that my comfort in our routines was only part of a much longer, much more complicated equation—one that had accrued several errors and would need to be fixed. Listening for any hint at all that we still had a future together even though our present was, it turns out, as tangible as the worlds she lost herself in every night.

But there was only silence. And when I woke up the next morning, there was no tea cup to wash.

***

We all have a tendency to imagine the worst, especially if the anxiety in our lives is heightened. I do this often, usually around how I'd feel if my wife exited my life for whatever reason.

What strikes me about these worries are the things around our house that would most remind me of her. We leave such strong impacts on the world just by interacting with it, and our relationships are no different. Aside from the obvious—the pictures from our wedding that hang out our walls, the clothes in her closet, the pages I've written about her—there are more subtle ways we leave breadcrumbs of ourselves in each others lives.

That's the genesis of this piece. I wanted to capture the routines that break when something changes or ends within a relationship. A favorite book that might lay out on a coffee table. A forgotten dirty glass. The small things that remind us that, holy shit, we're inextricably tied to someone else.

If my wife were to suddenly disappear from my life, I think those are the things I'd have the hardest time with. The things she does every day that impact me in almost imperceptible ways. Those nuances of her personality are the reason I love her to begin with. Their absence would be a devastating reminder of what I lost.

A SIXTEEN YEAR OLD'S LAMENT

I have to write this poem
But they don't tell you how
People are awestruck by
"My soul is as dark as night
When the autumn leaves fall from the sky"

But what meaning does that have?
To the billions dead
Because of unnamed gods
Or creature-borne diseases
The spread among us and from us
Like fleas on dogs

Actions speak louder than words
But the pen is mightier than the sword
In a world where children are left parentless
From random chance
To be raised by grandparents
Who know nothing else

A world of responsibility

Placed on the shoulders
Of a boy or a girl
Who aren't sure who they are
Or what they believe in
Or where they'll end up

Pressure paints pain
With ideologies so strong
Until that ideology and responsibility
Become a starvation for attention
In a self-destruction sort of way

These thoughts that everyone has
Spill from the pen in my hand
To rationalize the events
That separate the men from the boys
While leaving his inner-child alone
In an effort to protect innocence
Innocence shouldn't need protection

Yes I still believe in love
Maybe it's because I'm young
Maybe I can't see another reason to live
Or find something else to believe in

I'll sit and I'll wait
And I'll take a chance
On the human race
Until the day I die
Dreams empty, or fulfilled

***

When the title says that this poem was written by a sixteen year old, believe it. At least, I wrote the initial version of this poem somewhere in that time of my life. The reason I'm including a lightly edited version of it in this collection is because it's stuck with me over the past (nearly) 20 years as the first time I got in touch with something meaningful in my writing. The trademarks of my style first appeared here: confronting cliche (while leaning into it), a flair for the dramatic, an unfocused thought process, but also a strong visual language. This poem is objectively not good, but I love it anyway for what it tells me about who I was and who I became.

THE FINAL DAYS OF FLORENCE

The pain was gone. *That's strange,* Florence thought. For the last few weeks, her every waking moment had been filled with searing, debilitating pain, only ever bludgeoned (but never mitigated) by the medications that dripped from her IV.

On opening her eyes she found it stranger still to be looking down at herself from several feet above her bed. Overcome by a sudden sense of falling, she windmilled her arms in an attempt at regaining her equilibrium.

"You haven't figured it out, yet, have you?" a tiny voice— nearly a whisper—came from near the doorway of the room. Florence turned toward it and found a goth-looking young woman standing there. She was tiny, child-like, and the paleness of her skin contrasted sharply against the deep black of her dress, hair, smokey eyes, and wings.

Wings?

"Oh no," Florence said.

"It's time," the Angel said, holding out her hand. "Come with me."

Florence looked back down at her body. She looked peaceful. Like she had finally fallen asleep after a long day in the warehouse where she spent 35 years busting her ass. The machines that monitored her vitals were quiet, with steady peaks and valleys. Her soul had exited, but her physical body remained alive.

She kicked her legs and pulled at the air, trying to swim closer to her body, but making no progress.

"What do you expect to happen right now?" the tiny woman asked, unmoved from the doorway, exasperation laced throughout her voice.

"My body is still functioning. Why can't I keep it?"

"Because your time is up. You're embarrassing yourself."

Florence stopped trying to pull herself back into her body and again glanced at the Angel. "I can't be the first person to do this?"

"Not at all. Everyone does," the Angel replied. "It's embarrassing to watch them, too."

Florence crossed her arms, defiant. "Fine. Aren't I at least supposed to see my life flash in front of my eyes or something?"

The Angel rolled her eyes. "Will that help you accept the situation so we can get going?"

Florence shrugged without saying anything. The Angel narrowed her eyes, then waved a hand.

Every moment of every year of Florence's life played out in front of her. Her birth, her parents, her loves, her husband, her son, her career, her friends, her mistakes, her regrets, her loneliness—everything she was in life unfolded in a kaleidoscope of colors and sounds and smells. She concurrently felt elated and depressed; loved and hated; fulfilled and empty. As she reached the end, it seemed the sum total of her life was a series of mistakes and major unfinished business.

Especially when it came to her son, Tony. She couldn't remember the last time they spoke. Sometime around when his daughter was born—maybe 20 years before? It felt wrong to leave him without at least attempting to mend that relationship.

"I need more time," Florence said, stopping the reverie before she reached its end (assuming it ended in this hospital room).

"You all need more time," the Angel said, an edge to her otherwise meek voice. "It's a flaw of humans that you never realize it during life. It's too late for that, now. Come with me, Florence. The transition will be easier if you willingly accept."

"And if I refuse?"

The Angel sighed, then fully spread her wings—they slammed against the walls—and leapt toward Florence. Florence thought that if she hadn't already died, she would have then from a heart attack. The Angel collided with Florence and together they went through the window like light through a prism. Before they could fly upwards (now that she thought of it, why did Heaven have to be up? Couldn't it be anywhere?) she fought the woman's grasp—thrashing wildly, screaming like a child not getting their way—doing whatever she could to impede the Angel's flight.

Florence felt her open hands connect with the Angel's face. She searched for the Angel's hair and, finding it, pulled with all of her strength. The Angel's grip loosened. Florence screamed again and tried to squirm out of the Angel's grasp, not letting go of her hair. The Angel let her go. Florence fell.

She landed on the roof of a house, sliding off its angled tiles to the ground. Florence felt no pain, but in her shock couldn't immediately move. The Angel came out of the sky like a bullet, her wings folded tightly by her sides. At the last second she pulled up and landed violently, but gracefully, on top of Florence's chest. The pressure the Angel applied to her chest felt like a night terror she couldn't wake from.

The Angel crouched to one knee and brought her face close to Florence's. "You're aggravating me."

"Good."

The Angel smiled. Florence didn't like that. In life she would have expected an Angel's smile to fill her with warmth and comfort. Instead, she felt like something bad was about to happen. "I'll make you a deal," the Angel said.

Florence tilted her head. In her long, difficult life she had learned that when someone with power over you offered a deal, you should listen closely. "What's that?"

"You get three days. After those three days, regardless of the outcome, you come with me. No fuss and no fighting."

With narrowed eyes, Florence asked, "What's the catch?"

"It won't easy. The rot inside of you won't be mitigated with any medication or remedy. You will feel every ounce of this decision in your bones and blood."

Florence thought about it. The medications hadn't done much for her recently, anyway, and if there was one sensation she had a cozy relationship with, it was pain. If anything, she thought she was getting off easy.

"Fine," Florence said. "I'll take that."

The Angel stood, releasing her. She reached out a small, alabaster hand. "Then we have a deal."

Florence took the hand and a warmth passed through her hand, up her arm, and rested in her spine.

The deal closed, the Angel fully spread her huge wings. She leapt into the air and disappeared over the buildings, a wake of air blowing what was left of Florence's thin hair into her eyes. Florence lost consciousness and fell backward.

***

Florence woke with a searing pain encompassing her entire being. It radiated out from her burning lungs. Every nerve-ending felt as if it was being pulled apart thread by thread. She tried to breathe in but that only made the pain worse.

Desperate for relief, she reached for the patient-controlled analgesia. Moving made it worse. Her skin felt taut, immobile, and she worried that if she moved too fast it would rip from her muscles. She pictured the flesh-colored ribbon unspooling onto the floor next to her bed. She snickered at the image. A mistake. The pain flared even higher, like fire given more oxygen.

Eyes watering, Florence opened her mouth to scream. A small whimper was all she could manage. She wondered why her body hadn't gone into shock. Was this what the Angel meant about feeling every ounce of her decision?

She fell back against her pillow, hoping that the pain would pass on its own and knowing that it wouldn't. After a few more minutes of debilitating hurt Florence was able to move. She wondered if it was because her body adjusted to her new situation, or if she had returned to a more normal state of discomfort. It didn't matter. Florence was glad to be able to breathe without feeling like she was inhaling glass shards.

Three days. That was all she had.

Her relationship with Tony had fallen apart nearly 40 years before. He was only 19 when she told him to leave. She had said it out of anger and frustration. At the time, she hadn't expected him to actually go. But he did, and aside from a few hesitant attempts to patch things up—him when his first child was born, her when her age and loneliness made her feel his absence—they hadn't spoken since.

Tony had inherited her stubbornness and his late father's propensity for grudges. To her lasting regret, she had done nothing to temper those things, instead focusing her energies on his fuck-up of a younger brother, Jake. Jake was a needy child, and became needier still after Mark died. At the time, she thought that if she didn't attend to him closely, he'd do great harm to himself and others. Even with her attention, he did harm.

But that had left Tony alone. And when Mark died, that meant he had to grieve alone. He acted out, not recklessly and dangerously like Jake, but in small (but no less destructive) ways. Drinking. Some drugs. An attitude that reflected her own failings. It made her hate him, and she knew he hated her.

Their emotions and tendencies were a corrosive, explosive combination the night he left. She was already irritated when he came home from work smelling of beer. She told him how disappointed his father would be in this behavior. He asked her what she cared, didn't Jake need a diaper change? Anyway, Mark would be alive if it weren't for her harassment. She drove him to a second job without contributing anything herself, stressed him enough that his heart gave out.

That was all it took. Florence couldn't remember what was said after that, but she did know that Tony left with only a small bag of his things and never returned for the rest. She wouldn't hear from him again for nearly 15 years.

There was a different pain now, this one a tightness in her chest that she knew well. It came whenever she thought of Tony. A sense of shame mixed with fear, and regret, and anger. A potent mix.

None of it mattered. Not now. All that mattered was that she only had another day and a half to make things right. She called the nurse.

"How are you today, Florence? Is everything okay?" the nurse asked after Florence waited for what felt like an eternity.

"Do you have a phonebook?"

The nurse cocked her head like a dumb puppy. "A phonebook?"

"That's what I said, yes. You know those big, thick books with people's phone numbers in them? I would like one."

The nurse furrowed her brow and bit her lip. From one stupid expression to another. She was probably trying to think of an excuse not to get Florence what she wanted. Let her try.

Florence would make her get it, eventually. "Yes," the nurse finally said. "I'll bring it to you." Florence sighed, grateful that the nurse didn't drag this our further.

She left and took almost a half hour to return. When she did, she placed the thick book on Florence's bedside table, next to the phone. "Can I help you find anyone?"

Florence struggled to lift the phonebook into her lap. She had to hide the pain that the strain caused her. Lifting the phonebook felt like every muscle would tear from her arms. "No. Thank you."

The nurse hesitated and Florence could see the question in her head. *Who do you want to call?* To Florence's relief, she didn't ask. The nurse nodded, then left.

Florence prayed that Tony was listed. So many people no longer even had landlines, let alone allowed themselves to be publicly listed. It only took a moment to find that he was still local. She dialed the number.

And waited as it rang. Once. Twice. Three times. Then four.

She wondered if he had Caller ID. Didn't everyone nowadays?

A young boy's voice answered. "Hello."

"Oh! Hello!" Florence said, excited. She didn't know that Tony had a second child—a boy.

"You have reached the Wachinski house. Please leave your name, number, and reason you called after the beep and we'll get back to you as soon as possible. Thank you."

Voicemail. Damn. "Tony, it's your mother. I would very much like to talk to you. I'm at Mercy hospital, so you can call me here or come visit me at Suite 402. Got a real nice set-up. Feel like a Hollywood actress, ya know? One of the famous ones, not a fuckin' B-lister. Alright, it'd be nice to hear from you. Please. Bye."

She could hear the desperation in her voice. And if she was aware of it, then Tony would be, too. Maybe even be frightened off by it. He'd sense that she wanted something the way meerkats sense danger.

No matter. Time was short, and she didn't trust he'd listen to the message. She dialed another number, this one already in her head.

"Ma? What's up?" Jake answered. His voice sounded an octave off and he formed words slowly. Slurred them. She knew he had been drinking, if not worse.

"I need you to do me a favor," she said, ignoring his compromised state. What good would it to do call him on it now, when he hadn't changed in the last 35 years?

"Yeah Ma, whatever you need."

"I need you to visit Tony. I want to talk to him." Even in his compromised state, Florence knew from the silence on the other end of the phone that he was thinking deeply about her request. "Are you still there?" she asked, hoping to spur a response.

"Yeah, Ma. I don't think he's going to want to talk to me."

"No shit, Jake. That's why you need to go to his house. He still lives on Eden. I looked it up in the phonebook."

"Can't you just call him or something?"

"Already did that. He didn't answer. Look, it's important, okay? Will you please just do this for me? Tell him I need to see him immediately and that I promise I won't take up more than an hour of his time."

"Fine. Okay. I'll let you know how it goes."

She thanked him and hung up, worried from the tone of his voice that he was planning on waiting a day and then telling her he went. Instead, he would spend the day high, watching reruns of Transformers and GI Joe. Florence needed a way to verify that he did what she asked.

What way was there to get a hold of an angel? The only way she knew of was prayer, which was something she hadn't taken seriously since childhood. Mark was a religious man and he forced her to prayer on occasion. But for her it was always pretend.

"What do you want?" a small voice asked from next to her.

Florence damn near jumped out of her skin. "How?" was all she could manage to say.

The Angel's wings rippled with her shrug. "I'm monitoring you in case you change your mind about coming with me." The Angel studied her. "But that's not what you were thinking."

"No," Florence admitted. She didn't understand why she felt guilty about that. Why should she give a shit if this lady wanted her to die? "I need your help."

The Angel rolled her eyes. "You want to change the terms of the deal?"

"No. I want a way to facilitate reaching the terms of our agreement," Florence said. She was proud of her phrasing. All those years of watching lawyer shows in her small apartment paying off. "I've asked my youngest son to reach out to Tony, but I don't have a way to check that he's actually doing it. Can you give me some way to watch him?"

"I can," the Angel said, her lips puckered as if she had just tasted something bitter. "If that'll help speed this up, I can."

"I think it will," Florence lied. She was skeptical that Jake would even go. And if he did, Tony wouldn't receive him in kindness.

"Okay," the Angel said. She placed a small hand over Florence's eyes.

***

When Florence opened them again it was the next day and she was looking at Jake from the passenger seat of his beat-up

Ford Focus. He looked terrible. She realized that when he came to visit her at the hospital he must clean himself up pretty good. Looking at him now—with his red-rimmed eyes, two-day stubble, gaunt face, and yellow teeth—she wondered if he went so far as to wear makeup on his visits.

Cigarette smoldering on his lips, Jake stared at the house across the street from where he had parked. The house was painted yellow (not unlike the yellow of Jake's teeth) and was in poor condition. The roof needed to be redone, the garden went untended, there were two exposed wires where the doorbell should be—all the signs of poverty in one small scene.

"Christ almighty," Florence said, embarrassed that neither of her sons seemed to be doing well. She remembered how much potential they had and wondered if she was the reason they squandered it. Probably more for Tony than Jake.

Jake sighed, then reached for the car door. Florence watched him cross the road and then—as if she were watching a movie that cut from a wide shot to a close-up—she was next to him on the porch. "Alright," he said to himself. "Asshole better answer."

He knocked and waited.

From the look on Jake's face, Florence almost felt guilty for asking him to do this. A small tremble went through his body. He looked on the verge of tears. He ground his teeth. She reached for his hand, implicitly understanding that she wasn't really there, and would offer no comfort. Story of her life, really.

Jake sighed and started to turn away, defeated. "No. Fuck that," he said, spinning back toward the door with a renewed strength. He knocked again, harder this time.

Florence smiled. For all his faults, Jake always found strength when it came to helping her. He never abandoned her, even when he should have. If she were capable of missing someone while in Heaven, she would surely miss him.

The lock on the door clicked. Jake reflexively took a step back. The heavy storm door opened with a slight *hiss.* "What do you want?" Tony asked from the other side, skepticism and paranoia in every crack of his face.

He looked better than Jake, but not by much. Florence could tell from his yellowed skin and teeth that he had spent much of the last 40 years under thumb of alcohol and nicotine. He had weight to him, though, and his eyes were as bright, sharp, and unforgiving as the day he left.

"Mom asked me to come," Jake said. His feet were should-length apart and he kept his hands near his hips—a defensive posture.

"I got her message. Tell her I'm sorry she's in the hospital, but we'll all be better off when she dies."

Jake—stupid, loyal Jake—stood up straighter. "How can you say that about Mom? I know you've had your differences, but—"

"But nothing, Jake. She kicked *me* out. She's never apologized for that. When I had Marnie I tried to fix our relationship, but she still never gave a fuck, even for her grandchild. So no, fuck her. She can rot in Hell. So can you."

Florence could see in the way Jake's face flushed red and he took a small step forward that he was losing his temper. Either Tony didn't notice, or didn't care. He had lost his temper at 19 and never found it.

"It's your own fucking fault you two fell out like that. Do you remember the things you called her that night? How you blamed her for Dad?"

"I didn't say anything that wasn't true. Now get the fuck off my porch. I don't want to see you again. You're worse than she is."

Although she didn't quite understand what form she was in, she knew she was crying somewhere. This pain was greater than any she'd felt recently. That's probably why that damned angel let her stay. This was the real test.

"She's dying, Tony! Don't you care even a little bit?"

"She didn't care about me when she was alive, why should I care that she's dying?"

Jake suddenly lashed out. His fist connected with Tony's chest. If it weren't for how unhealthy Jake was, he might have seriously hurt Tony, especially at his age. Instead, Tony took a step back, absorbed the blow, then rushed forward. Jake realized his mistake and tried to retreat, but his reflexes were too slow. Tony grabbed him by the arms, twisted his body, and threw him onto the porch.

"Ah, fuck!" Tony cried out. He held his lower back. "Jake, I'm this close to making you choke on what's left of your teeth. Get the fuck off my porch. Don't let me see you again."

Tony hurried back into the house and slammed the door. The lock clicked.

Florence knelt by her son. "I'm sorry I made you do this," she said.

Without recognition, Jake picked himself up, flicked his middle finger at the door, and went back to his car.

***

Jake was the worst messenger she could have chosen. But who else did she have? Old age was lonely. She had never had many friends to begin with, and the few she did trust were dead. Mindy passed 15 years prior in a car accident. Lucille to cancer not long after that. Katherine was still alive, but her Alzheimer's had stolen enough from her that it no longer mattered. Without Jake, Florence was truly and totally alone.

Which meant there was only one option.

As soon as the thought came into her head the pain started. Right in the center of her chest, then spreading outward like a great wave made of pinpricks, each cell in her body screamed in discomfort.

"Ignore it," Florence said to herself through grit teeth. At this point, what was physical pain to her? Was it worse than the pain of losing her husband barely 20 years into what could have been a 60-year marriage? Mark was her soulmate—she knew that then and had only become more convinced as she lived without him. As she started and abandoned relationships with other, lesser men. Was it worse than the loss of her sons? Tony to anger and apathy, Jake to drugs and mistakes.

No. This pain wasn't worse than what she had already lived through.

She lifted herself off the bed, every muscle in her body straining with the effort. Slowly, carefully, she placed one foot on the floor, wondering what would happen if she slipped and slammed her head into the end table. Surely she couldn't die more than once.

"I wouldn't do that to you," the Angel said from the corner. Her wings were folded around her so she would be small enough to fit into the chair. "But you may want to move a little faster. More than half your time's gone." The Angel smiled. Florence had never thought an angel could have a bad side to be on, but apparently she had accomplished the feat.

She shuffled from the bed and studied the various monitors that tracked her pulse and whatever else. "Fuck it," she said, and pulled all the sticky pads from her body. The monitors went quiet. Next was her clothes. Where were those?

"What are you doing?" someone asked from the doorway. A nurse.

"I'm leaving," Florence said.

The nurse didn't laugh, but Florence could see the amusement in her eyes. "I advise against that. Let me call Dr. Oberei, you can discuss it with him."

"I don't have time for that," Florence said. She tried to keep her voice calm and knew she was failing. The shakiness of each word as it left her tongue was apparent even to her. "Where are my clothes?"

The nurse pointed at a small dresser next to her. "You'll need to sign paperwork," she said.

"That's fine. Just make it quick."

The nurse left Florence to struggle with her clothes, alone and in pain.

Nearly an hour later, when Florence had finally made it to the nurses' desk and began signing the paperwork that would allow her to leave of her own volition, she wondered what hurt more—her insides or her hand from scrawling her signature so many times.

"Mrs. Wachinski, I can't stress enough how dangerous your leaving is," the nurse said.

"I know," Florence replied. "You've said it enough. Is this it?"

The nurse took the paperwork that Florence held out to her. "Yes," she said, sincere worry on her face. Florence felt bad for her attitude.

"I know you're concerned," Florence said. "But we both know I'm dying. I want to go out on my own terms and take care of some things I should have taken care of years ago."

The nurse shook her head. "I'll call you a cab."

And that was that. Another nurse sat Florence in a wheelchair and brought her to the hospital exit, where a taxi picked her up.

***

The further Florence got from the hospital the more pain she was in. As she moaned and whimpered in the back seat, the cab driver watched her with concern in his rearview mirror. She inhaled deeply, trying to manage the pain, and smiled at him.

"Don't get old," she said.

"I'll try not to," he replied.

The cab pulled in front of the poorly maintained yellow house she knew to be her son's. "You don't have to wait for me," she said as she handed the driver a wad of bills. She hadn't even bothered to count them. As a young woman her biggest dream was to not have to worry about money. If only she knew then that goal would only be realized after she had already died.

Florence stood on the sidewalk in front of Tony's house for a long time after the cab pulled away. What would she say? Would he even listen?

Slowly, painfully, she climbed the cement steps onto the wooden porch.

"Deep breaths," Florence told herself as she raised her frail hand to knock on the door. She breathed in through her nose, held it, and then out through her mouth. It didn't help with the pain, but it helped with the nerves.

She knocked. Her brittle knuckles felt like they might shatter with each rap. Would he even hear such a light knock?

There were footsteps on the other side of the door. She took a step back and closed her eyes, her imagination failing to picture what might happen next. The door opened slowly, like it was anxious.

"Hi. Can I help you?"

That wasn't Tony's voice. Florence opened her eyes. A tall, skinny boy no older than 15 stood in front of her. Her grandson.

Before the tears could fill her eyes she spoke, "Hi. Is your dad home?"

Conflict stained the boy's face. "He doesn't want to see you."

"You know who I am, then?" The boy nodded. "What's your name?"

"Peter."

"Hi Peter, I'm Florence. Your grandmother." Florence wasn't sure why she announced something he already knew, but felt like it was necessary. Like if she didn't say it, she wouldn't believe it herself.

He stared at her. She could see that he was deeply considering something and knew that he already had an impression of her inherited from his father. Probably a fair, but incomplete, one. "Okay," he finally said. "I have to go now."

And then he closed the door.

Florence waited, expecting Peter or Tony to have a change of heart. To invite her inside. Air out their dirty laundry. Allow her to die peacefully.

But after another ten minutes of standing on the porch, with every nerve ending in her body crying out for relief, she knew that wasn't going to happen. She became incensed.

"Tony Wachinski! The least you can do is give a dying old woman five minutes of your time! You stubborn sonofabitch. I won't leave until you talk to me! I'll sit right on this goddamn porch until I die, and you'll have to step over my rotting corpse to get to your car!"

Florence sat on the porch steps, alone in her pain, expecting her outburst to have some benefit. She was wrong. A half hour passed. Then an hour. Neighbors walked by the house and stared. Florence began to suspect that Tony might call the cops on her. That was fine. She'd fight them too. Never liked police, anyway.

Time didn't matter now, so Florence stopped checking her watch. It only reminded her of Mark, anyway. He had gotten it for their 10th anniversary and the only time it had left her wrist was when she showered or was in the hospital. The engraving on its back, "J+F" was nearly smoothed over after all the years of rubbing against her wrist.

Night came. She sat there with her pain on her son's porch, waiting for him or the Angel to come for her.

The door opened. Her heart filled as she turned around. It wasn't who she expected, or even hoped for, but she found herself more grateful for Peter. He stood in the doorway, a pillow and blankets in hand.

"Did your father tell you it's okay to bring me these?" Florence asked.

Peter ignored her. "You're both stubborn as hell," he said. "I don't want you to die on our porch."

"Don't worry, kid, I won't. Made a deal with an angel."

"I don't think angel's make deals," Peter said. "But okay." He handed her the blanket and set the pillow down beside her. "Are you hungry?"

Florence nodded.

"Give me a minute." He went back into the house. A few minutes later he returned with a plate of reheated pasta topped with grilled chicken and a white sauce. "Dad made this for dinner," he said.

"Is he a good cook?"

Peter shrugged. "He only has a few recipes, but they're pretty good. He likes to grill."

Florence smiled. "So did his father. Your grandfather." Peter stood awkwardly over her, watching her eat. "Don't be weird, kid, have a seat. I'll try to eat quick."

Peter sat next to her. He looked like Tony. Same nose, same eyes. But the shape of his face was different. Must be his mother's.

"Do you have a girlfriend?" Florence asked between bites of pasta.

"No," Peter said.

"Why not? You're a handsome kid."

"I don't know. There's a girl I like in school, but I doubt she likes me back."

"Have you asked her?"

"No."

"Then how would you know?"

"What if she doesn't like me? That's embarrassing."

"Why? She's not obligated to like you, just like you're not obligated to like anyone. Eventually, you'll find someone who does. But trust me, life's too short to wonder. You wanna hear about how I met your grandfather?"

Peter hesitated, like they were breaking some rule and the longer he sat with her the more likely they were to get caught. "Okay," he said.

"When I was your age I worked at our family store. Cash register, cleaning, the bullshit that no one else wanted to do. I noticed this young man was coming in everyday just to mill around. He rarely bought anything, and when he did he could barely look at me. I honestly thought he might be stealing, so one day I confronted him. I said, 'What's your deal?' He said he didn't have a deal. So I told him he needed to buy something or get out, and not to come in unless he needed something.

"He started to leave, but then turned around and looked me in the eye. He said, 'I think you're real pretty. That's why I come everyday. I like to look at you.' And then he left before I could tell him how stupid that was.

"He didn't come back for a few days and I felt bad for yelling at him. It hadn't occurred to me before he told me he thought I was pretty, but I thought he was cute, too. I was so wrapped up in my job that I hadn't even noticed I was attracted to him.

"After a week or so, he showed up again. This time, he immediately plucked something off the shelf—I'm not even sure he looked at what he was taking—and brought it up to the cash register. 'I'll go out with you,' I said before he even had to ask. From then on, he rode his bike to the store everyday and waited for me to finish work. The rest is history."

"All it took was for him to admit he thought you were pretty?" Peter asked.

"That's all it took." Peter nodded. Florence handed over her plate. "Will you visit me again?"

"Uh… yeah. Sure. I can do that."

Peter took her plate, went back inside, and Florence cried before she went to sleep on the hard porch.

***

That night Florence dreamt of Mark. He often appeared to her in dreams, taking her hand and walking through their memories together. This dream was different, though. Instead of memories, he pulled her in a different direction—into some imagined future they never had.

She sees them grow old together, and in that fantasy there is no reason for Tony to leave. Mark is able to control Jake (sometimes with a slap) and keep his darker urges at bay. Florence watches her sons grew up to be functional, well-adjusted adults and not the angry, bitter men they actually are.

With Mark's retirement income and social security, they retire to the suburbs. She sits next to him on the porch. He drinks tea and watches the neighborhood kids run past the house. She watches him. He turns to her and when he opens his mouth a small voice escapes, "Open your eyes Florence. Face your reality."

Florence's eyes sprung open, and with the flood of daylight so came the pain. She groaned and sat up slowly, her stiff old body fighting her for every inch. "God, you look like shit."

She turned toward the voice and found Tony sitting behind her, coffee in hand. "It's been hard to keep up my beauty routine at the hospital."

"Lucky it's summer. You wouldn't have lasted the night in the winter."

"Oh, I think you'd be surprised," Florence smiled. "I met Peter last night. He's a sweet boy."

"He is. Don't know where he got it from. Ain't from me. Definitely ain't from his mother."

"Where's Melissa?"

Tony sighed. "She's six years older than Peter, Ma. She joined the military. She's overseas right now."

"Oh. I hope she's doing okay."

"Doing as well as she can, I guess."

"Good. Good… Is that second cup for me?"

Tony grit his teeth and held it out to her. "I want you to go."

"I will. I just need you to hear me out, first."

"About what, Ma? What can you possibly say that would mean anything after all these years?"

"Tony, please. I don't have much longer."

"I know. And that makes it worse. The only thing that could spur you to reach out to me, to meet your other fuckin' grandkid, was dying. What am I supposed to do with that? Give a shit? 'Cause I don't."

Florence nodded. "You're right. I should have reached out. But you're so goddamn stubborn…"

"Right. It's my fault you didn't reach out. That tracks."

They were sliding into their old routine. The one that Florence established when Tony was a teenager. The one that led to her severing ties with him when he was only 19. Still a boy. And the one that would prevent her from getting closure before her death.

"No. It's my fault. All of it. I've had a lot of years to consider my actions, and having considered every angle, I want you to know that I accept the blame. I fucked up. Fucked up bad. After Mark died I needed to be strong for you. But I've never been strong. He was the strong one. And your brother needed so much attention. It's no excuse, I'm just trying to put you into my mindset. I was overwhelmed, and you were sad, and then angry, and I didn't know how to handle any of that. So I decided that the easiest thing to do was to let you go. I've always regretted it."

Tony stared at her for a long time. "Are you done with that?" he asked, pointing his chin at the cup in her hand. She had yet to take a sip.

"No," she said.

"Okay. Leave it next to the door when you go." He opened the screen door to step inside.

"That's it?"

Tony paused, halfway into the house. "Is there more?"

"You don't have a response?"

He sighed and stepped back onto the porch. "There is nothing you can say to make me forgive you. That time passed when Melissa was born and you didn't even send a congratulations. The only reason I came out here this morning was to get you the fuck off my porch." He turned back to the house. "And if you talk to Jake again, tell him I want grandma's fucking jewelry back, if he hasn't already smoked it. That was supposed to go to my daughter."

And then he was gone. Florence wasn't sure what she had expected. She supposed that he had at least listened to her. She had accomplished her goal. So why didn't it feel like it?

"Are you ready now?" a small voice said from above her.

"Can I have a sip of this coffee?"

"Hell no."

She felt a tug on her hair and was yanked out of her body, which lay back in the hospital bed. "Thank you for bringing my body back here," she said.

"I didn't do it for you. That man's dealt with enough of your bullshit."

It hurt, but Florence deserved it. "Do I get to see Mark again?"

The Angel frowned at her. "Where do you think you're going?"

"Can't blame a girl for hoping."

"There's a difference between hope and delusion," the Demon said. "By the way, your grandson is right. Angels don't make deals with people.

*****

My grandmother died when I was in college. I didn't know her well, we had only met a few times in my life, and at the time I had a lot of feelings. Anger and grief, mostly, not because she was dying but because she was never a part of my life. There were lots of reasons for that, none to do with me, but it always felt like a lost opportunity for our family.

My father and sister visited her in the hospital without me. I wanted to go on my own. The only conversation I can remember having with her was in that hospital room. She told me about her husband, my grandfather (who had died long before I was born) and asked me questions about my life. It was a pleasant, relatively short conversation.

Afterward, I wondered if she wanted things to be different. If, given the opportunity, she would make amends and put more effort into being a part of her grandchildrens' lives. This story was initially born of those thoughts.

The first draft I wrote then centered on the grandchild. In other words, it was ego-centric to my experience and my feelings at the time. One of my creative writing teachers read it and asked, "Why is she so focused on her grandson when the other family members are more important?" That teacher was right.

I rewrote the story from scratch, not even consulting the original version written all those years ago, for this collection. I've always liked the idea and Florence as a character (I can't say it's based on anything but the loosest sense of my grandmother since I didn't know her) and so I wanted to approach it with time, distance, and a different emotional maturity. In the end, it's actually a bit more cynical and mean-spirited than the original work. But it's also more fun, interesting, and focused.

As for how much of it is still autobiographical—the answer is not too much. Broad strokes, a few small details, but mostly I was shooting for an emotional honesty.

YOUR ANGER

The droplets of sweat at the edge of his receding hairline
Boil away under the heat of your anger

I think about how one day we're all going to die
And the moments like these,
The small moments of emotion
That daily seep from our souls like a slow drip
And over time spill out
From our eyes and our mouths
In great waves of crying and yelling
Don't mean anything at the end

I wonder, as you sit and radiate your loathing
So red in the face, so warm to the touch
If you'll even remember this in a year's time
Or, more likely, if this is one more forgotten footnote
In a reference book written in a different era
When we were young
And is nary consulted
Except for when we need a hit of nostalgia

THROUGH DARK INTO LIGHT

Like he needed a hit of nicotine

The term of your anger has always impressed me
Your rage is a closed loop
Emotion made perpetual motion
You pace
Holding yourself and trembling
I feel the energy inside of you
Seep into the room
You are ready to explode

I know all this of you because I feel it too
We are helpless
Watching our father gargle
His last few pained, wheezing, cancerous breaths
Like a man slowly drowning

I check off all the same tired clichés as you
He's too young
I'm not ready to lose him
He did this to himself
It's not fair

And just like you, I reach the same conclusion
Just die already

For there is a part of us
Beneath the anger
That is bored and fed up
With the inconsideration of someone
Who makes you wait for him to die

I could be writing or gardening
Or something that feels productive

You could be dancing or drinking
Or whatever it is you like best
At a minimum we could not be thinking these thoughts
In a shit-smelling hospital room
On a weekday afternoon

Yet here we are
We watch our father's emaciated soul
Drain from his body
Without even a cup to catch the drops
Instead, our anger evaporates
The damp thing into the air
Lost
Until it eventually disintegrates
Into its base molecules
And, like his decomposing body
Rejoins the Earth
And is remade into something new
And, one can hope
Something better

***

I don't remember exactly when I wrote this poem. It was a long time ago, but also not so long ago. It's not based in any real situation (my father is still alive and well, thank the gods old and new), but the emotion is real. Specifically, both of my parents smoked like chimneys, though my father has since quit. And I kept thinking about how my sister and I would feel if their health failed and they ended up suffering in a hospital. The strength of that emotion led to the first draft of this. From there I applied the water metaphor and refined the language a bit until it became what it is.

THE PASSENGER

Part of me felt guilty for treating my father's corpse like the family furniture, but his cancer had been a drain on the family's finances. A laborer his entire life, my father never had good insurance, and he had gotten sick too young for Medicare. In these ways, he had slipped through society's gaps. Absent the ability to give him a king's burial, the least we could do was honor his wish of being buried with my grandparents in Buffalo. Even if it meant cutting corners on *how* that happened. Like transporting his body in a U-Haul instead of paying the thousands of dollars to have the funeral home do it.

Avoiding the highways—and asshole drivers that might rear-end me, cameras, speed traps, and state troopers—meant leaving late in the day and driving overnight. I would take the Leesburg Pike out of Virginia and drive East-to-West through rural Maryland, Pennsylvania, and New York. Surprisingly, the drive wouldn't take much longer than if I had risked the interstate. I hoped that maybe it'd even be a bit more scenic and peaceful.

Dad's passing had left me in a confusing emotional state. Grief, anger, disappointment, frustration, panic, worry, and relief all swirled in my gut and chest. He was sick for a long time. Me and my sister, Erica, had lost a lot of sleep and a lot of time at work visiting him and worrying about him. We were drained emotionally and financially.

After the funeral I planned to get blackout drunk for as long as it took to move on.

Once away from the last vestiges of civilization, the boredom creeped in. Out here, the radio offered more static than listening options. It was still light out, although the shadows of the trees lining the road were already long, and eventually the repeating lines of farms and cows and horses lost their novelty. Just outside Middletown, Maryland, is when my mind first wandered. The last time I had seen my father healthy was over a year before. Erica had asked me to come to the house to move cinderblocks she was using for a landscaping project. As always, Dad played the role of supervisor. He looked terrible. Gaunt and pale, with black marks beneath his eyes, I suggested he see a doctor.

"For what?" the old man asked.

"To get checked out. Something's wrong," I had said. Erica had glared at me, which I later learned meant *I've had this conversation with him a hundred times. Drop it.*

Dad waved the suggestion away. "I'm fine," he said. "Just haven't been sleeping well. Focus on what you're doing."

A month later the only way I would be able to see him was in the hospital surrounded by the doctors he had so desperately wanted to avoid.

"C'mon kid, eyes on the road."

I looked toward the tall, thin man with the white beard in the passenger seat. "I know," I said. "Sorry."

"You looking to join me back there?" my father asked, pointing toward the U-haul's storage compartment.

"That's not funny."

"Wasn't a joke. How're you holding up?"

I shrugged. If my father were actually alive and sitting next to me I'd say I was fine and leave it at that. Practice the art of avoidance he had mastered. But Dad wasn't alive.

"Why wouldn't you just go to the doctor?" I asked. "Maybe we could have found the cancer sooner. Done something to fight it. Maybe you'd still be here."

"C'mon Derek, you know it was already too late for any of that. Was I supposed to go on chemo or something, spend the next however many years sicker than a rabid dog before dying anyway? No thanks."

"How you went was better?"

"Dunno. But it was on my terms. I don't think a man can ask for much more."

My voice rose. "If you'd have just quit smoking earlier. Saw a doctor more than once every fifteen years. Done anything to care for yourself." I blinked back tears. Whatever this was— ghost or grief—I didn't want it to see me cry. "We could be at Erica's playing cards or something right now."

Dad snickered. "We both know that ain't how this would've played out. If I were still alive you'd be at home, doing whatever it is you like to do when you're alone. Before I got sick we saw each other—what?—twice in three months? You ain't even live that far away."

"I didn't see you make much of an effort. You didn't even bother to call me. Why should I be the one to make the effort? I'm your kid!"

Dad looked down and stared into his open hands, like he was trying to palm-read himself. "Why would you want an old man bothering you? You and your sister have both grown past me in lots of ways. I know I've been nothin' but a burden for a long time."

"What?" I asked. I felt frustrated heat radiating off my face. "Why would you think that?"

"'Cuz it's the truth."

"Whatever. That's in your head. If you ask me, your kid is always your kid. Don't matter if they grow past you or not, or if you think you're a burden. You should want to be there."

"You think I didn't want to be there?"

"Didn't seem like it. Not for a long time."

I stole a glance back to the passenger seat, but Dad was gone. Just like him to cut bait when the conversation got tough.

***

Nothing eventful happened through the rest of Maryland. The road just continued on, farms and trees blurring together into a looping scene of deep browns and reds intermingling with shadows. I had long since given up messing with the radio, so my only accompaniment was the sounds of the U-haul and the light October drizzle pattering on the windows.

I stopped for food in Orbisonia, Pennsylvania. There was no rush, after all. Erica's flight into Buffalo didn't land until the morning, so I had nowhere to be for her. The plan was for me to go directly to the funeral home, where I would drop off the body for dressing before the viewing in two days.

Right off my route was a pizza place. I parked in the little lot and hesitated before going inside. Scenarios ranging from his U-haul being stolen (what a surprise that would be for the thief!) to locking myself out of the van and needing to call for help ran through my head.

Overthinking. That's all this was. I double-checked that I had the keys in hand before locking the doors, then chose a seat next to a window overlooking the lot.

"Hi," my waitress said just as I was settling into my seat.

"I need a minute," I said with an edge to my voice. "I just sat down."

"Cool it," my Dad said from across the table. I looked up at him and he was frowning. "She's just doing her job."

I looked from him to the waitress. She was a young woman, no older than 15, with a nose stud, tattooed hands, and dyed raven-black hair whose roots shown blonde. She was in the middle of rebelling against something, and the only way to do so in a town this small was to try becoming someone new.

"No problem," she said. "I'll check back in soon."

"I'm sorry," I said. "I don't mean to be an asshole. It's just been a long night."

She nodded. "I deal with assholes all the time and I've seen worse. Can I start you with something to drink?"

"Coffee, please," I said. Without caffeine I had doubts that I'd make it all the way to Buffalo.

"Coming right up. I'll give you a minute to look at the menu."

She left me without losing her smile. I liked that. Despite her outward appearance, she had a sweet demeanor. When she did come back I ordered two slices of mushroom pizza. It was all I could afford with any money left for a tip. I wished that I'd be able to spare more of one.

The coffee was bad, bitter and burnt. The pizza only slightly better. But they did fill my gut. While I ate I ruminated on all the fights with my father over the years. There was the one when he was drunk and couldn't figure out how to change the TV input from HDMI to cable and blamed me for breaking it. For such a small thing, it was the closest we had ever come to blows. Too young to drive, I stormed from the house, slammed the door, and ran down the street. I came home late that night, when I was sure that Dad was asleep. The next morning neither of us said anything about it. I wonder if we should have. I wonder if communicating more would have changed anything in the long run.

I had moved out as soon as I could. The fights were less frequent after that. I'm not sure if that's because distance makes the heart grow fonder, or because age sands our sharpest edges down. It doesn't matter. What matters is that we fought less, though not never. Anger is something inherited, and it's been passed down generation-to-generation in my family.

Just as I was getting up to pay at the little counter near the door, a police car pulled up next to the U-Haul. A cop got out and circled the van. My stomach dropped. I worried I would puke and lose what little nutrition I had gotten from this cheap meal.

"Relax, kid," my father said, suddenly next to me. "Panic will only make things worse. Take a breath, pretend nothing's out of sorts, and keep moving forward."

I leaned against the counter, keeping my body turned to keep an eye on the cop, and waited to be cashed out. The cop peered into the U-haul windows, then leaned against the hood and lit a cigarette. What a town.

"Leaving already?" my waitress asked.

"Yeah. Just passing through. Do all the cops around here lean on other people's vehicles to smoke?"

She peered past me and her features hardened with irritation. "Only the power-hungry assholes. He'll give you some shit, but if you ignore him you'll be fine. He's probably just bored."

I nodded, grateful for her insight, but pissed off that I'd have to deal with this guy. I signed the receipt, staring at the line that read 'tip.' Doing the math in my head, I figured out the maximum I could give her from my bank account without risking overdraw fees. "I'm sorry I can't leave you a bigger tip," I said.

Without looking at the receipt, my waitress shook her head. "Around here any tip is a good one. Stay safe out there."

I turned away, prepared to confront the cop waiting outside. "Keep your cool," my father said. "If you're cool, he'll be cool." I wished I had a count of the number of times Dad had said something like that to me, despite how hypocritical it was. I struggled to manage my anger because his own actions had taught me that the world was built to inconvenience us and that every inconvenience is a personal slight. Even this trip was an inconvenience because my family had the audacity to be poor.

The best course of action, I decided, was to pretend I didn't even see the cop. I passed by him, feeling the ugly man's eyes and smelling his wafting cigarette smoke, keys crushed in the fist I kept hidden in my jacket pocket.

"Moving in?" the cop asked.

I glanced at him without interrupting my momentum toward the van door. "No," I said. "Just passing through."

"Where from? Where to?"

None of your fucking business. I'd already be gone if you weren't bothering me. "Cool it," my father said, keeping in step with me. "Just answer his questions and he'll leave you alone."

You're one to talk, I thought. *Where was this zen attitude while you were alive?* Dad shrugged. "Do as I say, not as I do."

I forced a smile at the cop. "DC to Buffalo."

The cop nodded, sucked the cigarette down to the filter, then dropped it into a puddle. "What for?"

"Funeral. Father passed."

"Sorry to hear that. Strange thing to rent a U-haul for a funeral, though."

I wanted to scream. In anger at this cop, yes, but mostly in frustration with myself. Can't even lie decent.

"Cheaper than renting a car out of DC, believe it or not," I said. I tried my best disarming smile and, catching a glimpse of myself in the U-haul window, knew how unconvincing it was.

Having answered the cop's question, I slid the keys into the van's lock. *Click.* I opened the door when the cop put a rough hand on my shoulder.

"Look, I believe you're just passing through and ain't here to do nothing untoward. But I need to take a peek in the back."

The back of my head tingled.

"Easy…" my father said. He was back in the passenger seat, his hands up in a 'stop' signal.

"What for?" I asked.

"It's just that there's been a lot of drugs flowing through here the past few years. Opioid crisis and all that. A U-Haul seems like a good way to transport that trash. And your story about renting this to go to a funeral smells like a pile of fresh bullshit."

"You think I'm transporting opioids?"

"Dunno. But the fact that you've decided to take the backroads from DC to Buffalo seems suspect, ya know? Like you were hoping to avoid running into any cops. If you ask me, it's suspicious enough to warrant probable cause for a search."

"No," I said. "You want to search my vehicle, get a warrant. Otherwise, stop harassing me."

I put my leg into the driver's side and the cop put one hand on the door and the other on his sidearm. "Don't need a warrant," he said. "So why don't you come on out here and open up that back door for me. If what you're telling me is true, ain't nothing to worry about. You'll be on your way in ten minutes."

I looked toward the passenger seat for guidance. Dad shook his head, just as lost as me.

"Taylor!" a voice called. The cop looked toward it. My waitress, her head peeking out of the doorway, looked disgusted. "Leave that poor man alone. He ain't done anything worth concerning yourself over."

"Girl, don't bother me while I'm working."

"Get the fuck out of here, Taylor. You're just bothering him because you're bored. You run out of porn to watch on your phone or something? Let him go on."

The cop, Taylor, stared at my waitress for a long time. She held his gaze. Finally, he frowned and shook his head. "Get moving," he said. "I'll escort you out of town."

He skulked away. I waved at the waitress, never more grateful for anyone in my life.

As promised, the cop followed me to the town line, but braked and turned away before crossing over. I hoped that would be the last of his bad luck even if, deep down, I knew there was more coming.

***

Stopping had gotten me into trouble, so I decided to drive straight through the rest of the way. Not that there was anywhere to stop. Once I passed into the northern part of Pennsylvania there was only one decent sized town. The rest was state park. First Moshannon State Forest and then, as I neared the New York state line, Allegany State Park.

Allegany held good memories. Before Mom passed we took a vacation there every few years, when enough time had passed for my parents to save the vacation time and money to afford it. Camping was the only time I can remember seeing my parents relaxed. It's also maybe the last time I saw my father truly happy. With Mom, and away from the worries and stresses of work, and bills, and raising two teenagers that were close in age, Dad actually smiled and showed patience. When Mom died the trips stopped. Life switched to survival mode.

"Dad?" I called out. I glanced toward the passenger seat. Dad sat there, expectant.

"What's up, kid?"

"What do we do now?"

"Same thing you've been doing. Keep on keepin' on."

"Things feel different. How are we supposed to just go on without you or Mom?"

Dad smiled at me. Before he had gotten sick, he had replaced his teeth with dentures. This apparition, or hallucination, or whatever this was had its real teeth. "I thought the same thing when your mom died. For years after she passed, I struggled. I struggled with drinking, and anger, and wishing I could see her, again. Some days were better than others. But the one thing that kept me going, that gave me hope, was you and your sister. Be there for each other and you'll make it through. Then one day, I hope, we'll all be together again."

"You think you'll see Mom again?"

"I do."

"Why haven't you gone?"

"I need to take care of you and Erica, first. Then I'll go."

Something about the words and the way he said them—so full of tenderness and genuine love—filled my heart. The emotion spilled over and I began to cry.

A few miles later I finally exited the storm that had followed me since Virginia.

***

About an hour and a half outside of Buffalo, in Kill Buck, NY the tire on the U-Haul blew.

I was on a narrow, two-lane road with nothing but forest for miles in any direction. I pulled off to the side of the road, hugging the tree line as closely as I could so as not to be side-swiped and forced to pay for damage to the U-Haul, since I hadn't sprung for the optional insurance (and damn sure couldn't afford a rise in premium on my own).

"Damnit…" I muttered as I dragged myself from the U-Haul to survey the damage. Night had fallen hours ago. The temperature had noticeably dropped. In short, conditions weren't ideal.

Although I'm not religious, I found myself mouthing a silent prayer that there was a spare tire beneath the U-Haul. If not, I'd have to call a tow and buy one. With what money I wasn't sure. Maybe I'd get lucky and find the only tow on Earth that took I.O.U.s?

On my hands and knees, I used the flashlight on my phone to peer beneath the van. To my pleasant surprise, there was a spare tire attached to the bottom of the vehicle. If I could find the tools I needed in the back, I could be on the road in a half hour.

I stepped to the back of the van and hesitated. Behind the cargo doors was my father's body. Although I had been driving this entire time with the sole purpose of bringing him to his final resting place, and knew in abstract that I had to protect it, I hadn't given a lot of thought to the physical body lying in the back of the U-Haul.

With a deep breath, I looked around me to be sure no stray vehicles were coming. A gray, beaten up pickup sped by. When it was safely out of sight, I opened the door.

The casket was a cheap wood. Temporary. His real casket was in Buffalo.

I climbed up on the ledge of the van and shut the doors enough that anyone driving by wouldn't be able to see inside. I knelt near the casket, placing a tender hand on top, tempted to slide it open.

"Don't," the ghost said from the other side of the casket.

"I know," I said. "I miss you."

"You'll feel that a long time. But right now you've got a job to do. The tools are over there." He raised his chin toward the corner of the U-Haul.

I found the jack and toolkit. I had to use the data on my phone to watch a short video on how to use it all, but within fifteen minutes I had successfully liberated the spare tire from beneath the van. In another ten minutes I had the van jacked up and the flat tire off the axel.

I was reaching for the spare when a rusted, sagging gray pickup truck slowed to a stop behind the U-haul. It looked familiar.

A young, clean-shaven man poked his head out of the driver-side window. In the dim moonlight (there were no streetlights on this road) I could see that his face was pock-marked, and a long thin bald spot marked where he had a scar cresting from the side of his skull to the tip of his ear. "Need help, friend?"

"No. I've got it under control. Almost done."

The man opened his truck's door and jumped down. He wore a thick hunter's jacket over a dirty black t-shirt, paired with jeans that had deep brown splotches on them. Probably oil, but the paranoia hidden deep in my brain wondered if it could be blood. Paranoia or not, I didn't want this guy near me.

"Pretty dark tonight. If I help ya it'll go that much faster."

"Thanks, but the hard part's over. No offense, but the only thing slowing me down right now is you."

The man smiled. I was surprised at how clean and straight his teeth were. They gleamed in the light coming from his truck's interior. The man didn't stop coming toward me. I glanced at the toolset that I had used to get the tire down from beneath the U-haul. I had left it near the back door of the van and this guy was close enough now that it wouldn't be difficult for him to cut off my path if I dove for a weapon. My blood pressure spiked.

"Everything alright, friend?" the man asked, hands in the air like I was pointing a gun at him. If only.

"No. A stranger offering help I don't want on an empty road in the dark is making me nervous."

The man let his hands drop into the pockets of his coat. My imagination flashed with images of getting stabbed. I pictured the knife entering my skin. The half-second delay before my blood would begin to leak from the wound. The immense pain that would freeze my body, making me that much more vulnerable.

I took a step backward.

"No need to be nervous, friend. Just offering a bit of help. Can't tell ya how many times I've stumbled on people like you in this road, here, helpless. Ain't a good way to be."

The man took another step forward. Then another. His pace quickened.

I panicked, first stepping backward to run, then thinking maybe I should fight. I spun around and the man was on top of me, grabbing at my jacket and pulling so that I fell on the ground next to the open driver-side door, my head missing its sharp edge by inches.

"You should've just accepted my help, friend. No need to be rude about it."

He slid a pocket knife from his jacket. The blade swung open and pressed against my throat. "Please," I pleaded. "I'm just trying to get my father home."

"What the fuck does that even mean?"

I closed his eyes, surprised to feel a tear slide down my cheek. I thought of Erica receiving the news that her brother was murdered on the way to delivering their father to his funeral. I pictured the devastation on her face. "I'm sorry," I said, aloud.

Suddenly, the pressure of the knife lifted. The weight of the man on my back disappeared. Sitting up, I turned over and saw my father standing in front of the man, a fully realized physical being. Standing tall and straight, Dad had his hand inside the man's chest. The man had gone pale, shuffling backward inconsequentially, and then it was over. The man dropped to the ground, dead.

Dad came to me. "It's alright, kid. I've got you," he said.

The grief came again, overwhelming me. Dad sat next to me, arm around shoulders, and held me for the last time.

***

The funeral was a small, somber affair. The family that was left in Buffalo numbered only a few, but that didn't matter. What mattered was that Dad was reunited with his parents in the cemetery, and if his spirit was to be believed, reunited with Mom somewhere else.

Me and Erica stayed with an aunt after the funeral. That night, when everyone had finished reminiscing and gone to sleep, I told Erica everything that had happened.

"He appeared to you?" she asked. I couldn't tell from her tone why she phrased the question that way.

"Yeah. Whenever I was in trouble or needed something."

She started to cry. "He was there for me, too. During the funeral preparations I was a mess. Whenever I got overwhelmed he showed up and calmed me down."

I smiled. "I asked him why he hadn't gone on, yet. He told me it was because he wasn't done taking care of us."

"I hope he feels like he's done enough, now."

***

It's inevitable that one day our parents will die. Some earlier than others. I'm lucky to have reached an age where I've become independent and had my own child while both of my parents were there to offer guidance and support. But there is also a lingering feeling that won't be the case for much longer. My parents are nearer the end of their lives than the beginning, which means my relationship with them is nearer its end than its beginning.

My father and I are close and although we haven't spent much time together over the past few years due to my moving to a different state and the COVID-19 pandemic stealing a year of our lives in 2020, I still can't imagine my life without him. This story, then, is my way of writing us a proper ending.

156

CLICHÉD GOODBYE

"What's the most clichéd goodbye you can think of?" Eddie asked.

Moses plucked a long blade of grass and stuck it in his mouth. He thought for a moment, squinting out across the wide field toward the setting sun. "This is goodbye for now, but not forever."

Eddie smiled. "That's a good one." He grabbed Moses's arm tightly. "No matter what happens, know that I'll always be with you… in here." He poked Moses in the chest.

"Little dramatic for me."

"There is a chance I could die."

"At boot camp? Seems unlikely. Maybe after, but I'll see you again before that."

"Fine. What about our fellowship has ended?"

"What fellowship? It's just the two of us."

"A fellowship can't be two people?"

Moses shook his head. "Na. Three at a minimum. I believe ideal fellowship size is around nine."

"Okay. I got it. How about it's been real, it's been fun…"

Moses picked up the end of the sentence, finishing it with Eddie. "… it hasn't been real fun."

A quiet as long and deep and beautiful as the sunset they watched settled between them. Both lost in nostalgic thought, neither feeling the need to vocalize the memories. Moses looked down at Eddie's hand. After Eddie had poked him in the chest he had let it drop to the ground near his own. Their fingers almost touched.

"It's gonna be weird around here without you," Moses said, after a while.

"You don't know that," Eddie replied. He leaned forward, moving his hand away from Moses's to absent-mindedly touch the grass between his knees. "You'll wake up tomorrow, shit, shower, and shave, go to work, come home, go to sleep, then do it all again the day after that. You won't even notice I'm gone. And then in six months I'll be back."

Moses wondered if Eddie actually believed that. "Yeah, you're probably right. Closest friend since the fifth grade and I won't even notice he's gone."

Eddie smiled at him. "See? Told you."

A strange frustration rose in Moses. This moment felt important but Eddie wasn't treating it that way. What else would he expect? This is how Eddie dealt with everything uncomfortable. Jokes. Sarcasm. Deflection. Moses had learned to care about him so much despite that. Sometimes because of it. He reminded himself of that and his irritation melted away.

"Look," Moses said, taking his turn to stare at the grass between his legs. "I'll miss you, anyway."

Eddie sighed. He hadn't wanted to face those feelings. It was already hard enough to leave without them swelling up in his chest, giving him heartache. "I know, man. Same here."

Nothing else needed to be said. When the sun was nearly swallowed by the horizon, Eddie checked his watch.

"I should head home. Still need to pack."

"Army's gonna break you of that procrastination bullshit."

"They'll try."

The two friends stood and faced one another. Without the sun the air had already began to chill.

"You'll come back, right?" Moses asked.

Eddie affected a thick Austrian accent. "I'll be back."

"I'm serious."

Eddie's smile faded. Tears welled up in his eyes. He blinked them back as quickly as he could. "Yeah. Definitely. It's only temporary, man. I'll always come back."

Moses knew it wasn't true, but he chose to believe it, anyway.

"Alright. Good luck."

"Thanks."

They clasped hands and Eddie pulled Moses in for a hug. They held it for a long time, eventually sliding both arms around one another. Slowly pulling apart, their foreheads touched. Moses felt the anticipation in his stomach.

"Okay," Eddie said, pulling away. "See you in six months."

And then he was crossing the field. Moses saw him raise his arm to his eyes, wiping away tears. His own eyes watering, Moses watched Eddie until he disappeared over the curve of the hill, and then walked home himself.

***

The idea for this vignette is based on two things: 1) emotions I experienced moving away from my hometown and 2) a desire to write something inclusive, from a perspective other than my own.

I remember the days and weeks leading up to my leaving. It really felt like the end of something, and I wasn't sure at the time if I was ready for it to end. My roommate moved out of our apartment and I stood in his room and cried. I had a pow-wow with my closest friends at my going-away party where we reminisced and ignored the other people there. But what stayed with me was how quickly it felt like things moved on without me. I remember giving one of my best friends a hug goodbye as I packed up my truck to go and it felt like there was an attitude of, "Welp, bye." That's not to say he didn't care or wasn't feeling emotional, it's just to say that sometimes in life there are goodbyes that feel underwhelming.

The second thing I wanted to attempt with this vignette was to write about romantic love from a perspective that isn't well-represented. Love is love, and I want to write characters from all different walks of life. As a straight, middle-class white guy, my feelings on my place in portraying minority characters are complicated, but I also believe that people are people, and should be written as such. Yes, we all have nuances to our personalities, cultural differences that are difficult to capture without being fully immersed, but there are elements of the human experience that are universal. Like friends leaving to pursue the next chapter of their lives. And young, tentative love.

Acknowledgments

These stories are inspired by and have been critiqued by more people than I can honestly remember. I'll do my best, here, but these acknowledgments can never be fully complete.

My wife, Hanh, inspires me, gives me feedback, does some graphic design for me, and influences the way I think about the world. Parts of her are reflected in everything I write. Without her there is no me.

My long-time reader is Shayn Delph. He's the most well-read motherfucker I know, so when he tells me something isn't working I don't need to think about how to argue with him. He's right. That's all there is to it.

You may have noticed lots of stories about parents and family in this collection. My Dad, Mom, and sister—Michael, Katherine, and Marisa—painstakingly molded me into the man I am over the years. Things weren't always easy or necessarily good in our household, but we worked at it and we learned forgiveness for one another and are a tighter family now than ever before. I'm lucky to have them as inspiration and support.

About the Author

Craig Gusmann first decided to be a writer around eight years old. Back then he wrote about time machines, werewolves, and space travel. Now he writes about time machines, werewolves, and space travel but with more nuance. He currently lives just a hair outside of Philadelphia with his wife, son, and two cats.

He is the author of ANH NGUYEN AND THE DISCORDIAN, available in paperback and ebook. He also blogs, posts monthly stories, and keeps the internet flush with cat pictures at www.craiggusmann.com.